Tess

By:
G.E. Stills

Hot Ink Press
An Imprint of
Crushing Hearts and Black Butterfly Publishing
Algonquin, IL 60102

Tess

Edited By:
Annette M Guerriero

Cover Art
by
S.K. Whiteside

To my wife who both tolerates and urges my writing obsession ever forward. I know being married to an author is no easy task. I leave you alone for hours while I bang away on my keyboard, talk to my author friends, do research or sit in silence lost in thought about on of my stories.

CHAPTER
~ 1 ~

"Goodnight Tess," Steve hollered at her back when she walked through the dressing room exit door.

"Yeah, sure asshole," she grumbled under her breath as she looked at the watch on her wrist and saw it was close to 4 am.

Bad enough it's nearly three when we get off anyway, but you just had to have a meeting after work.

After walking down the hallway a short distance she entered the employee locker room of *Fantasy Dreams*. Stopping in front of her locker, she took out her purse and put on her heavy jacket before leaving the room. Further down the hall she left through the employee exit. The blast of frigid air that met her caused her teeth to chatter and she wrapped the jacket tighter around her wishing she'd brought her longer coat.

Or at the very least long pants to change into.

She dug her car keys out of her purse before putting her hands in the pockets of her coat. At least her hands would warm up. There wasn't anything she could do about the freezing air that rushed up under her short skirt though. Her panty hose, and the thin material of her panties were not much help when the cold blast kissed her upper legs.

Damn, it wasn't even snowing when I came to work. Thank God I wore boots tonight at least. In only a few steps her eyes became watery in reaction to the bitterly cold air, and the tracks of her tears seemed to freeze to her cheeks. As quickly as possible she shuffled across the parking lot toward her car through a foot deep blanket of snow. Only a few cars were left on the lot because of the late hour

The lights of the parking lot reflected off the blanket of white, creating a contrast of brightness and deep shadows. Eerie silence surrounded her. Just before she reached her car, she pressed the key fob. The lights flashed and the door unlocked. Mentally she verified the location of her snow scraper in the car.

Start the car and then clear the windows. At least it will begin to warm up by the time I've finished. She shivered.

As she lifted the door handle someone shoved her forward. The action pinned her right hand against the cold metal of the door handle and trapped her other one still in her pocket.

A gravelly male voice as cold as the night air, spoke from behind her. "Got anything I want bitch?"

Her heart skipped a beat and then leaped to her throat in terror. *Oh God!*

Squirming and trying to push away from the car, she realized her struggles were useless. She had not heard the crunch of footsteps when they approached from behind. A moment later, pressure and something pointed plunged into her lower back just to the left of her spine and intense pain followed.

As more adrenaline surged into her, Tess's heart to race even faster. She knew without a doubt that she'd been stabbed. A scream of fright burst from her lips, splitting the silence. Moments later, her head snapped back as her assailant pulled her long hair exposing her neck. He produced a razor-sharp blade and sliced across her throat. The scream of terror she had just started became a gurgle as her blood flowed from the wound. All at once the weight of the man's body sandwiching her against the car, vanished.

Dropping her purse to the ground, her hands flew up to her neck as she tried in vain to staunch the gush of warm blood. Turning, she slid down the side of her car, hands still clutched futility to her throat. Her vision blurred as she scanned across the snow-covered lot seeking any type of help. Then from the corner of her eye she detected a flash of movement.

Tess sat, leaning against the car, looking at the crimson colored snow around her before falling face first into it. Blackness closed in, then there was nothing.

****

Alonzo peered down at the stricken woman, and then his gaze shifted to the mugger twenty feet away where he'd tossed him. Dropping to his knees, he pulled her up from her face down position in the snow. Brushing her hands from her throat he saw the terrible knife wound across it.

People die every day, he reminded himself. *Don't get involved. Still there is something about her.*

Rolling her to her back, he smoothed his hand over the wound and the deep cut closed. The bleeding slowed to a trickle and soon stopped altogether. He had just started searching for other wounds when his sensitive hearing detected a stirring from the direction of the mugger.

The man stood and brandished his knife. "I don't know who ya is but ya shuldnt a butted in. Now I'm gonna cut ya. I don't mind killin two."

In a flash of motion, Alonzo stood in front of the mugger. The man slashed out with his knife, intent of disemboweling Alonzo, but as fast as the knife thrust came, it was too slow. Alonzo's hand wrapped around the man's wrist, stopping his motion dead. With a growl, he squeezed the man's wrist and felt the satisfying crunch of bone.

The scream of pain and rage the mugger started cut short when Alonzo whipped his head back, sunk his teeth in the man's neck and ripped out his throat. Tossing the dead body to the snow, he whisked back

4

over to the injured woman and dropped to his knees. He placed his ungloved hand to her chest.

Yes, a heart beat, though it is very weak.

Placing his ear close, he heard her labored breathing. Tearing open her jacket, he reached under her blouse and ran his hands over her, searching for more wounds. He felt a slight stickiness on her stomach. Flipping her over, he felt much more on her back. Again his hands smoothed over her flesh and the wounds closed.

Now what? She's lost a lot of blood. She has to be very weak. If I leave her here, she'll freeze to death before an ambulance gets here. He stood up and looked down at her. *And when the EMTs examine her, they'll have a lot of unanswered questions about her rapidly healing wounds. If I was simply going to let her die, I screwed up.* He grimaced. *On the other hand, what else could I do? She brought me several rounds of drinks. What was her name? Tess? Yeah Tess. She talked a little each time she brought a round. I found her both vivacious and attractive. Sure she is nice but…Whatever, I'm going to do I need to do it fast before some of her fellow workers come out.*

Grabbing her out of the snow with one hand, he lifted her as if she weighed nothing. After fishing her keys out of the snow he also grabbed her purse. Opening the back door of her car, he placed her across the back seat. He looked at the bar exit, fearing that at any moment someone would come out and spot the dead man and himself. Using his arm, he quickly scrapped off the loose snow from the front and rear windows. Tossing her purse to the passenger seat and slipping behind the wheel of her car, he sped off. "Damn it," he cussed at himself in disgust and pulled over to the side a few blocks later.

He scrambled out of the car and opened the back door. After prying her mouth open, he slashed a fingernail across his wrist. Blood welled to the surface and he dribbled some of his blood in her mouth before the wound closed. He knew that the droplets of his blood would cause the healing system of her body to shift into high gear, rapidly replacing the blood it had lost. Climbing back behind the wheel he headed for Interstate 25.

He just finished leaving Denver when the sky began to lighten slightly in the east. The falling snow abated slightly by the time he reached Castel Rock. Looking down, he saw that the gas gauge read near empty.

"Figures." He snorted in disgust.

Pulling into an all-night gas station, he filled the car and headed south once more. He pulled over in a secluded rest area and checked Tess again. Feeling her forehead, he was pleased to find it warm, feverish, her body was hard at work healing itself.

At least her pulse is a little stronger and her breathing isn't as labored. He checked the trunk, and to his relief found a blanket neatly folded in one corner. Using it, he covered her.

Alonzo welcomed the grey cloudy dawn but the clouds threatened to break soon. Rummaging through her glove box he located a pair of sunglasses.

Pink female designed frames. *It figures. They couldn't be unisex ones. They'll just have to do.*

The roads were clear once he drove south of Colorado Springs. He increased his speed. The clouds broke and bright sunshine streamed into the car. Stretching the frames, he put the sunglasses on. He drove all day and into the night while Tess continued to sleep. Stopping in Albuquerque, he made a quick trip into a hardware store and picked up a few food items at a grocery store, before heading east through the mountain pass. Turning partway through, he headed north on highway 14. Deep in thought, he almost missed the narrow dirt road that led to his house.

Bundling the sleeping Tess over his shoulder, he went inside and laid her on the couch. He then crossed the room to light a fire. Starting with her boots, he removed all of her blood soaked clothing. He went to the bathroom and got a bowl of warm water along a washcloth so that he could give her a sponge bath. He washed her body until all traces of blood had been removed. She moaned slightly a few times but continued to sleep.

Just before he covered her with a clean blanket, he looked down on her naked form. She didn't have a dancer's body like many of the other women at *Fantasy Dreams*. The soft mounds of her breasts were large but not huge. From washing them and feeling them roll gently under his hands, he was certain they were natural. Her stomach had a slight bulge rather than being flat. Her hips flared a little wide and her thighs were maybe a little thick, but still she was very pretty. And that face. *God she has the face of an angel.* She had narrow eyebrows, long thick eyelashes, a thin nose, and luscious full lips. Long, feather-soft dark hair reached to her waist.

"Tess, you're a very beautiful woman. Maybe I should have let you perish back there in the snow, because now I need to figure out what the hell to do with you," he muttered in disgust.

Gliding silently into the bedroom, he turned down the covers before returning to the living room to pick her up. Going back into the bedroom, he gently placed her on the bed. Pulling the covers up around her, he then placed a dog collar around her neck and secured it with a length of chain. The other end of the chain locked to an eyebolt he had screwed into the wall.

As the fire spread its warmth through the house he refilled the bowl he had used to clean Tess and washed her blood from the leather couch. He gathered her blood soaked clothes and put them in the trash.

8

Finally, taking an extra blanket, he lay down on the couch and pulled it over him. Tossing and turning, he lay awake trying to decide what to do with Tess next. At last sleep came without him having reached a solution.

Alonzo started to wakefulness and looked around. Sunlight streamed through the French doors that opened onto the patio. A grin came to his face when he thought about the human fallacy of thinking his kind were restricted to the night. He knew most humans didn't even believe in his existence. Those that did, thought him forced to remain in darkness and sleep during the day. Yes, he found direct sunlight slightly uncomfortable if exposed to it for a lengthy time, but burst into flames. He grinned. *Hardly.*

He checked on Tess. She still slept. Her coloring looked better though. He went in to his bathroom, took a shower, then dressed. Standing beside the bed he sliced his wrist again and dribbled more of his blood into her mouth. After taking care of things around the house and talking to some business acquaintances on the phone, he made himself comfortable in the stuffed chair across the room from his bed, opened a book to read, and watched her.

A few hours later he heard her groan and saw her closed eyelids ripple. Putting his book down, he watched as she became further awake. Finally her eyes opened. She sat up in bed, her gaze darting from side to side in panic and confusion as she took in her new

9

location. Then, spotting him, they focused. Belatedly, she realized that in sitting up, the coverings had fallen, exposing her breasts. Reaching down she jerked them up to cover herself.

He watched the look in her eyes harden as she realized that she was not wearing so much as a stitch of clothing. Then she noticed the collar and chain.

"Hello. Welcome back. How are you feeling?" he asked.

Tess didn't say a word.

"God you have such fantastically beautiful hazel eyes. Are you hungry?"

She ignored his question and in a string of profanity, she started asking her own. "Who the hell are you? Where the hell am I? And where the fuck are my clothes? Why the hell am I chained up like a damn dog?"

"I think I'll wait to answer your questions until you've calmed down a little Tess. I'll ask again. Are you hungry?"

He saw recognition flood into her expression. "I remember you from the club. You were seated at one of my tables and I served you drinks. So what? Now you've kidnapped me? Did you rape me while I was out? Maybe you intend to rape me now. Maybe you get off on seeing a woman's look of fear when she is being raped."

He could feel his face heat in anger. "I didn't rape you before, and I don't plan on doing so now. I'm

10

going into the other room until you cool off a little. Think Tess. Think about what happened when you got off work and headed to your car. If you decide you are hungry… then call me." He got up abruptly, and slamming the door behind him, stormed into the living room.

****

Tess glared at the closed door as the memories started to return. Terrible memories. The feel of a knife stabbing into her back and then slicing across her throat. Blood. Lots of blood. Her blood. Sinking down to the ground while leaning against her car and then nothing.

She felt her throat and then her lower back. Nothing. No scabbing, not even scars. How could this be possible? The memories were so real. "Hey you. Whoever you are. I've got more questions to ask," she yelled at the closed door.

Maybe I should be careful. Maybe I shouldn't act so angry. He might stab me again. Fuck it. There are worse things than dying.

The door opened and he stood there silently.

"So you stabbed me. Do you intend to stab me again? Maybe you'll kill me this time."

"I didn't stab you Tess. Ask yourself this. If I had stabbed you, wouldn't it have been easier for me to just leave you there in the snow and let you die. Why would I have bothered to…heal you and bring you here? Tess, I don't want to hurt you."

11

In a voice that sounded much calmer than she felt, she went on. "Okay, so you say you didn't. Then who did? Why don't I have any wounds? Was it all my imagination?"

He walked in the door and sat in the chair again. "The man that stabbed you was named Skag. I've been following him for a while because of... maybe we'll go into why at a different time. It really doesn't concern you right now. He did stab your throat. That is not your imagination. I healed you. How... is a subject to be discussed at a later time."

Emboldened by his statement that he did not intend to harm her, she plunged ahead. "I hate to keep calling you, *hey you*. What's your name?"

"Alonzo, my name is Alonzo."

"Okay Alonzo, so why am I here, wherever here is? I'm lying here naked in your bed, I assume this is your bed, and chained to the fucking wall. That's not very encouraging to me. What do you intend to do with me?"

"I honestly don't know what to do with you at this time. It's complicated."

"So how about giving me back my clothes, letting me get dressed and we can sit down and talk about these *complications*."

"I can't, I can't give you your clothes—"

"Why not?" she asked indignantly.

"Tess they were covered in blood...your blood. The only thing that could be salvaged was your boots."

12

His statement hit home. In a quiet voice she went on, "So I'm to stay here naked in your bed until you decide what to do with me?"

"I'm sorry. I don't have any clothes to fit you. I don't have any women's clothes here. I guess you could wear one of my dress shirts if you wished."

After considering her choices briefly she answered. "That's better than nothing. That will be fine Alonzo. Please give me one to put on."

Getting up, he went to his closet, picked out a sky-blue one and handed it to her. "I'll step out of the room while you put it on."

She paused for a moment before responding, "There's no need to leave the room. Just close your eyes…or not, after all, you undressed me." her cheeks heated at that thought but she continued, "you've seen everything I have, so being shy is kind of silly. Beside you forget where I work and the outfit I have to wear. That doesn't conceal much."

He sat back in the chair and closed his eyes. Throwing back the covers she stood and put his shirt on. While she buttoned it she studied him.

Alonzo stood taller than her five and a half feet. She judged about six feet. He had dark features with shoulder length hair. Broad shoulders and a wide chest. His narrow waist gave way to strong muscular-looking legs. But the most striking thing she had noted about him were his fantastic grey eyes. Eyes that seemed to look into her very soul.

Finishing with the last button she said, "Okay, I'm dressed now. You can open your eyes. Did you say something about eating? I find that I'm pretty hungry."

"If I remove your chain will you promise not to try to escape? You won't be successful if you do, I assure you."

"For now. I just want something to eat. Okay?"

"Fair enough." He stepped close and removed the chain.

Chapter
~ 2 ~

"Follow me," he turned his back and walked toward the door.

Gee he doesn't worry much that I could attack him from behind and maybe overpower him.

As if he could read her mind he spoke over his shoulder. "If you're thinking of jumping me, don't. You will loose. I'm a lot stronger and faster than you are."

Arrogant prick.

"I wasn't thinking of it," she lied, "I just want something to eat."

They passed through a large living room. She noted it had two brown leather couches, two chairs, a fireplace and French doors. The room had a rustic and cozy looking décor. Wood beams ran across the ceiling and the wood floor was polished to mirror brightness. In addition to the door they were headed for and the French doors, there were three others. The doorway across the room opened into a bright and spacious kitchen filled with more stainless steel appliances than she had ever dreamed of owning.

He directed her to a seat at the breakfast nook. After pouring her a glass of milk he set a peach and grapes in front of her.

"Sorry. I don't have much to offer in the way of food. I wasn't expecting company."

"You could always let me go," she suggested, knowing it wouldn't happen.

He snorted and chuckled. "Nice try. No, that's not going to happen right now. I'll go to the store. Make a list of the things you like."

He handed her a piece of paper.

She poised the pen over the slip of paper. "Just how long do you plan on keeping me here? Do I need to make a long or short list?"

"A while."

"Not very talkative are you."

"No."

She made a list of things she liked to eat. After pushing the list towards him, they studied each other for a few moments.

When she finished eating he stood up. "I have to leave for a while. Come."

"Come," she mimicked in indignation. "I'm not a damn dog."

"Very well, I misspoke. Please follow me." He spun to face the door.

I might not have another chance like this. When he turned his back she struck. Jumping on him from behind, her fists hammered on his head and shoulders trying to drive Alonzo to the floor, but it was no use.

The next thing she knew, he'd plucked her from his back and held her in front of him at arms length. One of his hands held the shirt bunched up, just under her breasts while her feet dangled in the air, still kicking helplessly. Her hands grasped at his arm futilely as she tried to break free of his grip. *It's useless*, she told herself. *His arm is like steel.* His free hand bunched into a fist and lay at his side. He shook her like a rag doll. His jaw locked in anger. Speaking through clenched teeth he growled, "Tess, I warned you not to try this. I could break you in half like a toothpick. I'm more than what I appear."

She watched in horror as his beautiful grey eyes turned blood-red and his mouth opened, revealing sharp looking fangs. Shock, fear and dread consumed her. She could feel the emotions march across her face.

"What… Oh God. What the hell are you?" she asked in a trembling voice, filled with the terror she felt.

"I'm a vampire Tess—"

"Vampires don't exist," she squeaked.

With no humor at all he chuckled. "And yet one dangles you helplessly in front of him. What is your explanation for the position you find yourself in?"

"Oh Jesus. I don't have one. Please Alonzo I'm sorry. Don't kill me. Please," she pleaded, tears streaming down her face.

He set her feet on the floor, still holding her shirt bunched. "I told you that I don't want to harm you, but don't test me. Now, shall we continue into the bedroom?"

"Yes," she mumbled shaking with fright.

The redness in his eyes faded away and he closed his mouth. He released his grip and turned toward the bedroom again.

Meekly, she followed and he chained her up once more. In a calm voice he told her, "The chain is long enough for you to go to the restroom or even take a shower if you wish. It's long enough that you can go into the living room, sit on the couch and watch TV if you like. I'll be back later." He turned on his heel.

Frozen in shock and fear, she watched Alonzo leave the room, while waiting for her racing heartbeat to slow. She heard a door open and close and assumed he'd left. Dashing to the bedroom window, she pulled open the heavy curtains and looked out.

Across a short clearing she saw trees, nothing but seemingly endless evergreen trees. Glancing to one side, she watched Alonzo switching cars around. He pulled a custom van out from inside a two-car garage and drove her compact in to take its place. Just before the garage door closed, she saw the back end of a shiny

18

blue sports car. After closing the garage doors he drove away in the van.

She let her gaze roam over the outside view again. Trees, nothing but trees everywhere she looked. Pea-sized gravel covered the clearing in front of the cabin and garage. A narrow drive led into the trees. *I must be somewhere in the mountains but where?*

Disheartened by her current situation, she went to the full-length mirror and checked her collar. *No way I'm getting that off.* Getting down on her knees, she examined the eyebolt screwed into the wall. *No way out there either, not without tools.* Frustrated, she decided to take a shower and check her wounds. Standing under the warm stream, she examined herself. She couldn't find any evidence of ever being stabbed or cut. Not even a scar.

That's just plain weird.

After showering she plugged in the blow dryer and using his brush, combed her hair dry. Shrugging the shirt back on, she fastened the buttons. With nothing else to do, she sat on the bed, leaned back against the rail and crossed her arms under her breasts.

So now what?

In her mind, she went over and over everything she could remember about the events leading up to this point. A sudden chill raced though her when she remembered being forced against the cold metal of her car. The terrible pain of having the knife stab into her back and then the blood gushing out of her sliced

19

throat. She shuddered. Still weak from blood loss she slid down, rolled over on her stomach and fell into exhausted sleep.

****

Alonzo drove to town and did his shopping, picking up the items she had put on the list and some items she had not. Going into a woman's boutique he went shopping for clothes.

"So what size does your lady friend wear?" the sales clerk asked.

"Ah… I don't know for sure."

"Okay…is she bigger or smaller in the chest department than me?'

"Um a little bigger." He felt his cheeks get hot.

The clerk smiled and her eyes twinkled. "Okay, she has bigger boobs. And what about here," the woman smiled and put her hands on her hips.

"About the same."

"Okay."

When he'd finished, he had an assortment of clothes and underwear. When the clerk finished ringing up the sale she smiled. "Thank you sir. I like the colors you picked out and the selections you made. Your girlfriend is a lucky lady. Not very many men would take the time to shop for their girlfriend like this. I hope I guessed the right sizes. If not she can always exchange or return them."

"Thank you Miss. You've been very helpful. I really appreciate your time and extra effort." He gathered up the bags and just before he left he turned to the clerk. "I really do appreciate your efforts. Here's a little something to express that appreciation."

He grabbed her hand and pressed a bill into it then walked out of the store before she could protest. *I hope a hundred dollars tells you just how much appreciation I feel.*

On his last stop he went to a butcher he knew and picked up the bags of cow blood as per their arrangement.

The sun had set before he got home. Darkness shrouded the cabin's interior. Switching on lights in the living room and kitchen as he walked through, he put the groceries away and then went into his bedroom. When he flipped on the light there he saw she was sleeping and that his shirt had ridden up around her waist revealing the soft cheeks of her butt along with her shapely well-toned legs. He set the bags of clothes on the floor and quietly tiptoed into the bathroom. There he stocked the toiletries he'd purchased for her.

I had to guess. I hope you like the body lotions and bath washes I've selected.

After making one last stop to cover her with an extra blanket, he turned off the light and left the room.

After making his bed on the couch he clicked off items in his mind. *The police will find Skag's body. They'll discover that Tess is missing and DNA samples of her blood will tell them that she suffered foul play. They'll think that Skag had an accomplice, hopefully.*

21

There won't be any evidence connecting me to the crime scene. I don't leave any. One of the advantages of being what I am. My fingerprints and DNA samples will have vanished long before they start checking.

Sleep eluded him once again. He got up, went into the kitchen and fixed himself a drink. Returning to the couch, he sat down, took a swallow of his whiskey sour and let his thoughts continue.

So, next question. What the hell am I going to do with her? I can't just kill her. She's an innocent woman. At the same time, I can't just set her free. She's seen far too much. She can identify me. I don't know how much she saw when I killed Skag but… Tess you're a dilemma. I guess I'll just have to keep you here for a while until I come up with a solution.

****

Tess's eyes flashed open and for a moment she looked around in confusion. Fingering the collar around her neck, the memories returned. A soft blanket covered her. She remembered it hadn't been there when she went to sleep earlier.

So he's back. I wonder what time it is. Those heavy curtains over the windows make it hard to tell if it's day or night.

Reaching out, she flipped on the lamp and rolled over. She felt a lot stronger than she had the previous day. Looking around the room, right away she spotted the numerous shopping bags on the floor across from the bed.

She recognized the name of the stores on them. Ones she only dreamed of being able to shop at. Curiosity got the best of her fear, and climbing out of the bed, she strode over to them and peeked inside. The bags were filled with women's clothing.

Either he has a wife or girlfriend that I've seen no evidence of, or these clothes are for me. Which is presumptuous on my part.

She jumped when his voice spoke from behind her. "I hope you like the things I picked out. If they don't fit then I can exchange them." Slipping a key from around his neck, he crossed the room and removed the chain attached to her collar. He then retreated to the doorway. "Remember yesterday, don't try to run for the door. You won't make it." Changing the topic he continued. "I'm going to fix breakfast for us. Oatmeal and toast. In the mean time, you can look through the selections and see what you think."

She turned and looked toward the door but he was already gone. Gathering up the bags she took them across the room and spread the clothes out on the bed. Skirts, blouses, a few pairs of blue jeans, stockings, bras and panties. "Nice clothes Alonzo." She glanced at some of the clothing labels. "Very nice! Damn!"

She noted that none of the panties were simple cotton briefs. The bras were not simple white ones either. "I'm more than a little confused here Alonzo. You keep me here a prisoner, chained up like a dog and yet you go out and buy nice clothes for me."

23

No answer.

"What's your game Alonzo?"

No answer

"Judging from the number of outfits here I feel like maybe you plan on keeping me here for quite awhile. I'm not happy about that."

She was not surprised when he failed to answer.

She cast a wistful look at the clothes and whispered, "I guess I might as well wear some of them. It's that or run around in his shirt." Picking up a pair of thong panties she smiled. Every item of the large selection was equally scanty in nature.

"Okay, I guess I can live with this. You forget what I do for a living Alonzo. I parade around half naked serving drinks. These outfits aren't any more revealing than what Steve makes me wear at the club."

She slipped the panties on, finding they fit perfectly. Next she put on a bra. The blue jean skirt fit a little snug but not uncomfortably. She slipped on a halter-top and buttoned it, completing the outfit she picked. Looking at the foot of the bed she spotted her boots and put them on. Next she went to the bathroom and discovered that he'd purchased more than the clothes. When she finished getting ready, she stopped at the bedroom door and called out.

"Alonzo, I'm coming out. I'm not making a run for the door."

Slowly, so as not alarm him if he watched, she crossed the living room and headed for the kitchen.

From the corner of her eye she glanced at the double doors, which she assumed, led to the entrance. She debated making a break for a second, but she cast the thought aside when she remembered what he was and how fast and strong he was too. She stopped at the kitchen entrance and he looked up at her.

"Wow you look very nice Tess."

"Thank you sir. You picked these things out I remind you."

"They're just clothes Tess. You're what makes them look nice."

Compliments from my captor? I'm so confused. Okay, try this?

"Now if I just had some makeup."

She watched him roll his eyes and he sighed. "Make me another list. A detailed one. I don't know anything about makeup items."

"Or you could simply take me with you and let me choose them."

His smug grin told her everything; he didn't have to say the words.

"I guess that isn't going to happen though is it?"

She returned his infectious grin. *On top of everything he's so damn handsome.*

"If I leave you unchained there will be no repeats of yesterday I trust."

"No repeat. I promise. Consider me suitably intimidated."

"Good, let's eat."

"Why are you being so nice to me? I'm getting mixed signals here Alonzo. On the one hand you go out and buy me a bunch of nice clothes. *Really* nice clothes. On the other hand you're keeping me a prisoner here. Am I a prisoner? What did I do wrong?"

"You didn't do anything wrong, but you saw things. I don't know how much you saw, but I can't take a chance that you'll tell anybody. I'd rather think of you as an unexpected guest here that's staying for an extended visit."

Laughing, she answered, "O–kay, an unexpected guest that is not at liberty to end her visit."

"Yep. Now let's eat, shall we?

She picked up her spoon and started to eat. At the same time she noticed him eating.

"Another belief about vampires bites the dust. You're eating."

"We can eat, although it's not necessary. I'm doing it more to make you feel comfortable."

"Thanks."

While they ate, she asked, "I noticed that you bought a swimsuit for me. Either you intend for me to freeze my butt off outside sunbathing or maybe there's a public pool nearby. Do you plan on taking me to a pool or something?"

"Or something. Eat."

"Not very informative are you?"

"Nope. Eat."

"I'm famished. Guess I didn't realize just how hungry I was." She finished her second bowl and the pineapple slices he'd laid out.

"Your body needs nourishment. It's still recovering from your ordeal. Are you ready to see the rest of the house?"

"Sure." *Taking me on a tour of his house? I don't understand. I'm a captive here and yet he is being so nice to me.*

He took her by the hand and led her into the living room. "The French doors lead onto a covered patio deck. It's a little cold out there right now. I'll show you out there later."

The touch of his hand caused strange but wonderful things to happen to her. She was somewhat uncomfortable, but she couldn't ignore the deliciously warm feelings at her core. They crossed and went through a door into a hallway. He opened a door to his right and showed her a smaller bedroom. "The next door down on this side opens into another bedroom."

"If you have all these extra bedrooms why are you sleeping on the couch? Oh, never mind," she finished when the reason dawned on her.

Grinning, he opened a door on his left and she saw a large, well-equipped office with bookcases that covered three walls, all filled.

"Wow. I guess you read a lot."

"Yes, I enjoy reading."

The last door on the left led into another bathroom.

"Nice house."

"Thanks." Again he took her by the hand, led her back across the living room and through the other door she had not been through. They stood in a foyer. Across the room were double doors she guessed led outside. On their left were stairs leading down. Going down the steps he flipped on a light switch set in a panel of other switches.

Her mouth dropped open when she gazed around the large room. One side had a collection of exercise equipment and game tables. The large swimming pool on her left grabbed her attention. Lounge chairs lined both sides. Large slanted widows formed the ceiling and let sunshine stream in.

"Wow," she said and then gaped some more. "I thought your kind didn't like the sun much." She finally managed.

"There's a lot you don't know about *my kind.*" He laughed.

"This house is huge for one person." She looked at the number of lounge chairs that lined both sides of the pool. "Unless there's more than one person that…." She left the sentence unfinished and cocked an eyebrow.

"Nice fishing Tess." He grinned. "I'm not married and don't have a girlfriend. I live here alone. I do entertain though. Others of *my kind* visit occasionally. So you see this is where you can wear your swimsuit."

Now why do I care if he's married or has a girlfriend? Why do I find that I'm thinking less and less about getting away and more about getting to know him better?

"When can I go…swimming that is?"

"Anytime you wish, so long as I'm here and you're not chained."

She ignored the being *chained* part of his sentence. Looking at the inviting pool she asked, "how about now."

"Anytime."

"Then if you'll excuse me."

"Don't try to go outside," he called after her.

"I won't. Remember, I'm intimidated," she called over her shoulder as she rushed upstairs. *It's frightening when I think of what he is. At the same time he's being so kind to me. No man has ever treated me like this. And this house, wow. It's fantastic. Sure puts my tiny apartment to shame*

.

Chapter
~ 3 ~

Changing into her swimsuit and wrapping a sarong around her waist, she raced back down stairs. She noted that he'd taken a seat in one of the chairs. Removing her sarong, she draped it over the chair next to his and sauntered to the edge of the pool with her back to him.

"I hope you enjoy seeing my bare ass. Just remember, you're the one that bought this thong cut 'kini."

"I think your ass is beautiful Tess. I think all of you is beautiful."

God did he just say what I thought I heard? That he thinks I'm beautiful?

She dove into the pool and swam underwater to the other side before she surfaced. Clinging to the side she faced him.

Can he see me blushing from way over here?

"The water is so nice. Do vampires swim? Or do they sink to the bottom like a stone? I mean everything I thought I knew about them turns out to be wrong," she teased.

"We swim."

"Then what about joining me in your pool?"

"Would that make you happy?"

"It might not make me giddy, I'm still a guest that isn't free to leave remember, but it would make me happy--er."

"Then I'll change and be right back."

He climbed the stairs giving her a chance to regain her color and calm the butterflies that were suddenly going crazy in her stomach. No man had ever called her beautiful.

"Da—yum," she said under her breath when he came back down. "What a handsome hunk he is. I knew he had a good looking face but da—yum."

A smattering of curly chest hair nestled between his well-defined pectorals. Broad shoulders gave way to well muscled biceps. A washboard stomach led into a narrow waist and strong athletic legs.

Turn around Alonzo. I want to see that cute little ass of yours again. She swallowed hard. *Suddenly I find that I don't much want to escape after all. Maybe I'll just stick around, enjoy the view, and see what he has planned for me.*

"Talk about beauty. My God Alonzo, you're a beautiful hunk of man," she whispered.

He poised on the edge of the pool. His leg muscles rippled with power as he prepared to dive. He swam underwater and surfaced right next to her.

"Happy--er now?" he asked.

Not even close. Back away and let me look at you some more. Then I'll definitely be happier.

"Yes, thanks," she said.

"What do you say we do a few laps? By the time we finish, the sun should be shining through the glass just right for getting a tan."

"Sounds fine to me Alonzo."

Swimming until she became exhausted, she climbed out of the pool and fell into a lounge chair. *He's right, the sun feels fantastic.* She closed her eyes and sensed him take a seat beside her sometime later.

****

In the beginning she tried to keep track of how long she had been a "guest," but as the days blurred and became weeks she gave up entirely. Alonzo had started sleeping in one of the guest rooms, and had replaced her dog collar with a fancy one made of shiny silver. About an inch wide, her new collar was just as, if not more, secure than the original.

Tess fingered the silver ring. *It is better looking though.*

Alonzo only chained her now when he left the house or he slept. The rest of the time she had the run of the house. As she wandered around exploring, she

33

didn't find a single phone. *Apparently the cell phone he always carries is the only one.*

"Please don't go outside unless I'm with you," he had requested.

"And just when are you going to take me out there?" she asked. "I haven't been out of this house since I've been here."

"Soon. The weather will be nicer soon and then I'll take you outside."

Looking out the windows she watched the season change from winter to spring. She didn't know how long she'd been here but she knew it had been more than a few weeks. The snow melted, the trees that were not evergreens grew buds and then new leaves. Wild flowers started to grow. With the onset of spring her attitude toward Alonzo changed.

She began thinking of him as more of a friend than someone that had kidnapped her and held her here as a prisoner. Lying in bed with her head resting on a soft pillow she stared up at the ceiling sightlessly. *Stockholm syndrome?* Sleep refused to come. Her mind was too busy analyzing her life now. In the beginning the only thing she'd been able to think of was how too escape. Now that thought almost never occurred. Escape to what? Freedom? Freedom to return to her mundane former life? She snorted into the darkness when her thoughts turned to that life. Return to being a cocktail server at *Fantasy Dreams,* working for a boss whose main goal concerning her was to get into her pants. Not for a relationship but just as a conquest. *I don't think so thank you very much.*

During the six months she'd worked at the club, she watched Steve bed most of the women that worked there. Stupid women, they thought sleeping with the boss would get them ahead. It didn't. They were just another mark on his scorecard. It drove Steve crazy when she refused to play his game. It was just a matter of time before he would let her go if she continued to reject his advances. Of that she was certain. For one thing, she didn't fit his tastes.

I don't think I'm bad looking; I just don't have the Barbie Doll figure of perfection like many of his dancers.

Realistically she knew that once she gave in to him, should she do so, soon afterwards she would be looking for a new job.

None of the girls working at the club were what she would term close friends. They were more like acquaintances that she occasionally hung around with. She hadn't had a close friend since adolescence. Her parents were deceased and she had an older sister that she never saw. There was no one in her life.

Her thoughts turned once again to that night. The night her life had changed. The *meeting* that Steve had insisted on. Curiously there were only two people at the *meeting.* Him and her. It had been just another ploy he had dreamed up in an attempt to get in her pants. She knew that.

Her life here was so different. *Besides the whole 'can't leave' when I want and being chained to the wall, is it really so bad?* In addition to being so damn handsome and polite, she enjoyed being with Alonzo. They played together like two kids. He never got upset when she teased him. Laughed at her antics and pretended pouts. She flirted with him often, but to her chagrin he never flirted back.

When she rarely had temper fits he ignored them. If she got really angry, he simply left the room leaving her with her hands on her hips, glaring after him. This pissed her off even more, she knew it and worse yet, he knew it. He refused to argue with her, but instead left her alone, denying her his companionship.

That's the worst punishment he can dish out to me, and he damn well knows it. Far worse than fighting back or taking away material things. In a short time my anger fades and I'm searching for him.

"Damn infuriating man. You know just how to deal with me don't you?" She grinned into the darkness.

Reaching up, she ran her fingers over the silver collar that circled her neck. It no longer served as a reminder of her captive status. Largely because she knew she wasn't. The collar wasn't even attached to the chain. If she demanded that she be allowed to leave, she had little doubt he would now let her. He only secured the chain when he left for town and she knew that even then it was unnecessary.

Her fingers caressed it lovingly. It now signified to her that she belonged to him. That he owned her. Giggling, she compared it to a wedding band. *All right, so I can pretend.* She giggled again. *Still I've never belonged to a man before and the feeling of belonging to him is great.*

Her grin faded. *Now if he would just possess me in other ways. Ways that I would be more than happy to give to him.* Butterflies started to flutter in her stomach. She squeezed her legs together in an attempt the quiet the sudden feeling of warmth between them.

"Damn aggravating man. You'll never make the first move though will you? Even though I've hinted, sometimes blatantly, that if you made advances they would *not* be rejected. No, you'll force me to flaunt myself. Maybe if I throw myself down and pull you on top of me you'll get the hint. If I did that, would it be a strong enough message that I want to have sex with you?"

She reached between her legs and began to pleasure herself, realizing it was the only way she was going to get any rest. Thinking of Alonzo, she wasn't surprised at how wet she had already become. Fantasizing that it was his hands rubbing against her folds, and his fingers sliding into her, she came quickly. Though now sexually complete, she still longed for the real thing.

****

Most days became a routine, breakfast, exercise, swim, sunning, lunch, TV, or reading, then supper. Quite often in the evening he rented movies for them to watch together.

"I brought home another of your sappy chic flicks," he said and grinned.

And I suppose as always you're going to sit at the opposite end of the couch.

Sure enough he curled up as far from her as he could get and still share the couch. He watched the movie with her and when she started to cry in one of the sad parts he handed her a tissue to dry her tears.

"Thanks," she blubbered.

"I don't know why you insist on watching these tearjerkers. You always end up bawling like a baby."

"I like them," she managed between sobs.

He just shook his head and smiled. "And that's why I rent them. It's also why I keep the tissue box handy."

"Thank you Alonzo,' she murmured.

****

She had become an expert at table tennis, foosball and pool.

"Hey no fair," she said and stuck out her lip in a pout. He'd dashed across the end of the table using his super speed to hit the ping-pong ball she'd artfully hit so that it would just graze the table on the opposite side from him. "That's not fair at all using your super powers."

He grinned at her sheepishly and she stuck her tongue out at him making him laugh. "I'm sorry. You have every right to be angry at me."

Always a gentleman. Always so damn nice to me. If you don't at least kiss me pretty soon I think I'm going to scream.

" I'm a little tired. I think I'll go upstairs and go to bed." *And play with myself... again.*

"I'm sorry Tess. If it's something I did, I apologize."

It's not something you did... it's what you didn't and haven't done. Damn it

"No, it's nothing you did. I'm just tired is all." Setting her paddle on the table she headed upstairs.

One day he drove away in her car and returned later in a cab. When he came inside she confronted him.

"Where's my car? Where did you take it?"

Evasively he answered, "You don't need it anymore. When I decide to let you leave here I'll buy you a new one. End of discussion."

The expression on his face made it plain he wouldn't talk about it anymore. She decided not to press, even though it made her angry.

The next day he left again. This time when he returned he had several sacks filled with clothes to add to her growing wardrobe. Taking out a fancy velvet box he handed it to her.

"What's this? Keys to a new car?" she asked sarcastically. As she'd gotten to know him better, her fear of him had evaporated.

"Guess you'll just have to open it and see," he replied smugly.

Flipping the lid open she gasped. Inside the box contained a diamond choker necklace and matching diamond earrings. Her eyes became misty. "They're beautiful," then she couldn't resist adding sarcastically, "To bad no one will see me wear them except a man that doesn't appreciate their true meaning…"

"What's that supposed to mean?"

Meaning I think this gift is so thoughtful on your part that I'm nearly in tears. Meaning I'd wear them in public proudly, especially knowing they had been given to me by a man that I think is the greatest.

"Nothing. I'll go try them on," she snapped. Turning, she marched for the bedroom.

"You've sure been moody lately Tess. Are you still mad about your car?" He said to her as she stormed up the stairs.

No, it's because you're the best thing that has ever happened in my life and I'm offering you the only thing I have to give you…myself. You're just too damn blind to see it. It's not a matter of you not wanting me either because I can see that you do in your eyes. "No, let me try things on and I'll model them for you if you wish," she called back down.

Standing in front of the mirror a growl of frustration rolled from her lips. She frowned and stamped a foot. When she put the jewelry on a smile replaced her frown.

They do look very nice. Thank you Alonzo.

She slipped on an outfit and upon entering the living room found him there. One after the other she modeled her new clothes for him but refrained from conversation other than in direct response to his questions.

"Thanks for all the new things, they're lovely. I'm tired. I'm going to bed. Goodnight." She shut the door behind her.

God he's always so nice to me and here I am acting like a bitch again.

The next morning over breakfast he said, "When we're finished here I'd like it if you dressed in shorts and comfortable walking shoes."

"Okay. May I ask why?"

"I'll tell when you finished dressing."

When she'd finished putting on shorts, a simple top and tennis shoes, she went back to meet him in the kitchen. To her surprise he took her hand and led her outdoors. "I think maybe you're suffering from house-a-tosis, would you like to go for a walk?"

At her nod he led her to a path. Still holding her hand, they strolled through the woods commenting on the things they encountered. He stopped frequently to ask if she was tired or if she wanted to continue on.

"Walk on," she answered each time.

Always, he took her hand again afterward. The simple act of holding hands with him had her stomach all aflutter. She wanted there to be so much more. To have him hold her, kiss her, and to make love to her.

Leaving the forest behind, they walked into a small field filled with beautiful wildflowers in countless colors. Their smell was fabulously intoxicating. Crossing through the field they stopped at the edge of a steep bluff. She gazed at the breathtaking view of the majestic mountains covered in green forest.

Casting a sideways glance at her companion, her heart skipped a beat. *The beauty here almost matches your handsomeness. Almost.*

"The view here is incredible Alonzo," she said in awe. "Absolutely incredible."

"I think so too. This is one of my favorite places."

"I can see why, it's—" She wanted to say romantic but instead finished with, "majestic."

She looked up into his fathomless grey eyes. She envisioned herself grazing her hands over his muscular chest and running her fingers through the curly black hair. The heat between her legs became nearly unbearable, and she could feel the wetness seep into her panties.

Throw me down and make passionate love to me right here… right now… among these colorful flowers, Alonzo. That thought only served to increase the ache between her legs.

God I've never wanted to make love to a man so damn bad in my entire life. The only thing I can think of is having his naked flesh pressed against mine.

She clung to his hand, certain he could feel the sweatiness of hers. When he spoke, her fantasy, like a soap bubble, popped and vanished.

"Tess…Regrettably, I've really disrupted your life. It's not fair for me to keep you around here against your will. I wish I felt comfortable just letting you go. Unfortunately I don't. Not because I think you'd intentionally reveal my secret, but you might say or do something that would lead to a lot of trouble for you…or me for that matter. How would you explain being gone for all this time just to suddenly reappear with no explanation?"

I don't want to leave. I've come to consider this my home. You treat me like I'm something special. Like I matter. There's just one thing missing in this wonderful new life I'm leading. That's what she wanted to say. Instead other words came from her mouth. "I understand. When we come up with a solution we'll address it then."

"Okay," he said, softly.

She averted her eyes and looked away to hide her silent sigh of defeat. What she wanted more than anything to happen here was not going to occur. "I think we should head back. I'm getting a little thirsty."

They strolled back to the house. She got a drink and fled to her room, angry and confused. "Damn you man. Don't you sense the vibes of desire I'm giving off?" she whispered. "Don't you find me desirable? You tell me I'm beautiful all the time."

All right Alonzo, we'll just find out how desirable you find me. She went to her closet, picked out a maroon mini skirt and button-up halter-top. Sitting on the bed she took up her sewing kit, *something else he purchased for me when I requested it,* she reminded herself and went to work.

After eating supper she went to her room again. She changed clothes and put on the earrings and necklace he'd gotten. In satisfaction, she watched him swallow hard when she came out of the bedroom. She'd shortened the hem of the already short skirt and taken in the blouse at the sides. The top was so tight it threatened to pop the buttons at any time.

"How about we play a little pool?" she asked.

"Ah…fine," he managed.

Barefoot and swaying her hips, she led the way downstairs. While they played pool, she waited for just the right opportunity, and was delighted when at last it came. Alonzo stood behind her when she leaned across the table preparing for a shot. Her breasts hung just inches above the felt. In satisfaction, she felt her skirt rise up in back and sensed his gaze on her.

"Alonzo are you looking up my skirt? Are you looking at my ass?" she asked.

44

"Um…maybe. So what if I am?" he growled.

Under the pretense of getting into a more comfortable position for her shot, she brushed against the table edge and felt her skirt rise even more. She could feel the cool air graze across her exposed lower butt cheeks in complete contrast to the heat between her legs. She knew her thong panties left her butt bare.

The brazen words slipped out before she even realized she said them. "Maybe you should touch and not just look."

Suddenly his hands were around her waist. A squeak of surprise escaped her lips when he quickly lifted her from her feet and spun her in the air to face him. For a moment, he set her back on her feet while his hands brushed up her thighs, pulling her skirt up until it was bunched around her waist. Lifting her again he seated her on the edge of the table and spread her legs wide while stepping in between them.

One look at the lustful need in his eyes sent the heat of her arousal burning straight to her core. She got warm and wet in anticipation. His lips first skated lightly against hers and then pressed hard, demanding. Her sexual arousal soared to even greater heights. Her scanty panties became soaked. His lips brushed against hers and then his tongue urged her mouth open. He fumbled with the buttons of her top.

Yes! Yes! A voice in her head screamed.

Her hands busied themselves unbuttoning his shirt. The last button of her blouse gave way and he

45

spread it to the sides. His hands glided across her breasts and then went to work on the clasp that held the cups of her bra together.

The last button of his shirt gave way and she slid it off his shoulders, letting it fall to the floor behind him. Breaking their kiss, he looked down and concentrated on parting her bra clasp.

"God you're so beautiful." His gaze fixed on her breasts. She knew her sequined bra held them tightly together creating a deep cleavage and pushing them up at the same time.

The clasp came loose, and he slipped the cups to the sides to join her open top, letting her breasts spill out. She moaned in pleasure when his hands cupped them, molded them, caressed them. He rolled her nipples between his thumbs and fingers until they became hard and stood erect.

Yes, yes, oh God yes, the voice in her mind cried out once more.

And then it was over. He stepped back. She watched the passion in his eyes fade. "We can't."

Why the hell not? The voice in her head screamed.

"I don't have a rubber." He supplied the answer to her mental question. "Vampires are supposed to be sterile but I'm afraid to chance it. I don't wish to get you pregnant. I'm sorry." Stooping down, he picked up his shirt, then turning on his heel, trudged up the stairs.

She sat for a moment, motionless while her racing heartbeat slowed. She slipped to the floor slowly and smoothed her skirt down while her eyes clouded over. She didn't even bother hooking her bra before she raced up the stairs. To her relief she saw that he was not in the living room. *Probably in his bedroom.* Fleeing into her room, she slammed the door behind her then tossed herself across the bed.

The tears that had threatened to fall now rolled down her cheeks in a torrent while she pounded the bed cover with her fists in both frustration and sadness. "Damn it, damn it, damn it!" she cried out over and over as the thought of what had almost happened played through her mind.

At breakfast they attempted to initiate conversation but failed. Neither one of them wanted to talk about the previous night. For most of the meal they sat in silence, unwilling to make eye contact. Finished, she went downstairs to exercise and he went to his office.

****

Closing the door behind him Alonzo sat back in his chair. He flipped open his phone, started to make a call, and then changing his mind, put it back in his pocket. "I don't much feel like talking to anyone," he mumbled to himself. Rolling his chair back, he left the office, got into his Porsche and drove away. He was halfway to Albuquerque when he remembered he had not secured her chain. "Screw it. If she leaves, then

47

fine. I almost had sex with her last night. I almost broke my promise to myself that I wouldn't. She's human and I'm two hundred and ninety-six years old. It would never work for us to be boyfriend and girlfriend and yet…"

All of the gallant promises he had made to himself were cast aside. The thought of living without her companionship, her fantastic personality, and her gorgeous looks made the prospect of a life without her look bleak at best. He knew he was ensnared in her web but had no desire to break free. Her allure held him as helpless as a fly in a spider web.

Face it Alonzo she's become a huge part of your life. She is a human and I'm a vampire, but suddenly that means nothing.

Most of the day he spent driving around town aimlessly. In the afternoon he stopped at one of the discount stores and made some purchases. As evening approached he got a pizza and headed home.

"Well, I guess I'll soon see if she's here or if she left while I was gone," he said as he pulled into the drive. "If she is still here I'll beg her to stay.

Chapter
~ 4 ~

Tess trudged up the steps to get a bottle of water and she heard the front doors close. Looking out the small side windows beside the doors, she watched his car drive away. "Good, run away. I don't want to be around you either." She turned and in a huff marched into the kitchen to get her water.

She sat at the kitchen table drinking the water and cooling off. Her clothes hung limp on her, covered in sweat. The hurt she felt from the night before had been replaced with anger. Anger at him and at herself.

I flaunted myself. Nearly threw myself at him. I acted like a damn horny slut just to be turned down. Damn you Alonzo.

Her anger stimulated her to an even more vigorous workout than usual. He was right; she didn't want to get pregnant. Certainly not under the current situation.

She had removed her expired birth control patch long ago and though he had been able to get tampons for her, he hadn't been able to get additional patches. With the new day she felt like a fool. She had nearly begged for sex only to be turned down. The fact that he was right not to have unprotected sex with her didn't help her mood any. She hated to admit she was wrong and he had been right. She hated to admit that her passion and desire had overwhelmed caution. Irritation with herself just added fuel to the fiery anger within her.

The doorbell rang. *What, did you forget your house keys when you ran away?* Storming to the door, she flung it open and her words of anger died in her throat. The couple facing her seemed as surprised as she. In panic she tried to slam the door, only to have the man stick out his hand and stop it effortlessly. He pushed it open with such force that it sent her skidding across the floor and slamming against the opposite wall, knocking the wind out of her.

The man came in and stood over her. He had shoulder length blond hair, was built nearly as well as Alonzo and stood even taller. "And just who are you my pretty?" He reached down with one hand, grabbed her t-shirt top and hauled her to her feet. But he didn't stop there. He lifted her up off the floor. He dangled her in the air at arms length and she looked into his eyes. Watery blue eyes that had a look of meanness in them.

The companion with him came into view. The woman had honey-blond shoulder length hair and a build she had often seen on the dancers at *Fantasy*

Dreams. Erect tits; no doubt augmented, a flat stomach and muscular legs. The clothing she wore was just as provocative as an exotic dancer's too.

The woman sniffed the air. "She's human." The woman's eyebrows arched. "Alonzo has come up in the world. No more cows blood for him. He's keeping a ready and renewable supply of blood handy all the time."

"Not very smart on his part to let *it* run loose when he's not here though." He walked into the living room carrying her at arms length and tossed her roughly on one of the couches. Tess curled up in a ball and trembled with fear.

He turned to the woman. "She's not bad looking either. No bad at all. Damn, I wish I had a setup like this. Drink from it, and fuck it. Makes me shiver with pleasure at the thought."

Turning to look down at her once more he added, "So tell me, do you taste good and fuck better? Maybe I should sample a little of both. You don't think Alonzo would mind do you Darla? I mean I share you with him don't I?

Darla answered, "I think you better not Jake. Alonzo just might kick your ass like he's done before." She laughed wickedly. "As for the sharing bit. I don't belong to you, so you aren't sharing me. When Alonzo and I fuck we do so because we want to and it has nothing to do with your sharing me."

Up until this point, Tess had remained silent, her voice frozen in horror. The thought of Jake biting and raping her raced through her mind. A loud scream of terror ripped from her throat. Roughly, Jake clamped his hand over her mouth.

"Shut up. Your screams annoy me. Darla, see if you can find some tape to shut this thing up."

"I'm not your slave Jake. If you want tape go find it yourself. I'll stay here and keep it silent though. Its screams annoy me too."

"Fine," Jake said in disgust.

Darla sat down beside her and Jake took his hand away. "Honey," Darla warned. "I'd advise you to shut-up. You're getting Jake a little angry. He just might do something that Alonzo will make him regret later, but it will be too late for you."

With a snort, Jake turned and stalked off to the kitchen.

"I don't know how valuable you are to Alonzo but he's a good friend of mine and I'll try to keep you safe from Jake until he returns," Darla whispered to her. "But you have to stay silent. Don't call attention to yourself while I try and distract him. Jake is not always a bad guy, but sometimes he thinks with the wrong head, if you know what I mean."

She looked up at Darla with a mixture of fear and hopefulness.

"So little slave, are you keeping Alonzo well satisfied?" Darla stroked her hand along her neck gliding her finger over its large vein, "And this too. I must confess to being a little jealous if you are. I wonder too just how good you must taste. I never pictured Alonzo as the type to keep a blood and sex slave."

Tess just stared at the woman in silence, remembering the warning Darla had given.

A few minutes later, with a roll of duct tape in hand and a bottle of wine in the other, Jake returned. Rolling her to her stomach, he pressed his knee between her shoulders, jerked her arms behind her back and taped them. Next, he yanked her legs upward and taped them. Grabbing her by the hair, he pulled her to her feet and snapped her head back painfully. After slapping a piece of tape over her mouth, he caressed one finger over her neck along her jugular.

"Such soft skin. Smooth and silky. Its racing heart is sending such a strong pulse through her vein here. So Inviting."

Using his grip on her hair, he spun her to face him. "Look at the wild fear in her eyes. Now that it's silent, I think I'll sample it and see how it tastes. Watch those eyes change and become dull when I drain its blood. Take it to the edge of death." A cruel smile split his lips and exposed his deadly fangs.

Turning his head, he faced Darla. "Oh don't worry. I won't drain it completely. I won't rob Alonzo of his toy. I just want to taste it and sample its pussy."

Her pounding heart sent fear and adrenaline coursing through her veins. She lay on the couch, helpless, with her arms and legs bound. She realized even if she were free, it would make little difference. Jake was incredibly strong. Any resistance she could muster would be worthless. It would only serve to anger him further.

Jake's clawed hand grasped the neck of her t-shirt and ripped downward, tearing the material and exposing her breasts. Hooking a hand under the waistband of her sweat bottoms, he tugged, rending the material easily. The torn material tumbled down her legs to settle on the tape that secured her ankles. Tess shuddered when Jake's finger glided over the thin material covering her sex. Brutally, he threw her on the couch where she curled up in a fetal ball, drawing her knees up against her chest. Jake started to unbuckle his belt and she knew the inevitable was about to happen.

Darla stood and placed herself in front of Jake. Pulling her top over her head, she bared her breasts. She grabbed the bottle from the table, opened it and poured some of the white wine over her tits. "Wouldn't you rather sample some of this?"

Reaching down, she ripped the Velcro closure of her short skirt open, letting the garment fall to the floor. She poured some of the wine over the thin material of her lace panties. Then, pulling the waistband forward she poured more on her pussy. "Or taste some of this?"

A deep growl rolled from Jakes throat. Tess watched as his lust filled gaze roamed over Darla's body. Saw him lick his lips and run his tongue over his fangs.

"Let's go swimming first and then let's fuck until we can't move." Darla grabbed Jake's hand in hers.

She watched as Darla guided him away. Darla placed his hand so that it cupped one cheek of her bare ass and wrapped hers around his shoulder. The two went through the door headed for the stairway.

Thank you Darla. Alonzo please come home. Please save me from this terrible monster. Please.

Struggling to her feet she hopped to her bedroom. Dropping to the floor she rolled under the bed. She was certain that if Jake searched for her, he'd find her quickly but she didn't know what else to do. Maybe by keeping out of sight and with Darla keeping him occupied, Alonzo would return before Jake found her. It was a slim hope, but the only one she had.

****

Alonzo drove up in front of the house and immediately spotted the car parked in front. He recognized it as belonging to Jake. He went into the living room and found no one. His gut clenched with a bad feeling. Darla, he was certain would be no problem around Tess, but Jake… He didn't much care for Jake and he definitely didn't trust him.

55

Then he heard noises coming from the basement. Loud drunken voices. At the bottom of the stairs he saw that Jake and Darla were on the floor screwing but didn't spot Tess anywhere.

Crossing the floor in a flash he came to a stop standing over them. "Where is she?" he demanded.

For the first time the two of them noticed him. "She's right here. Can't you see me fucking the hell out of her? Don't worry Alonzo old boy you know Darla. When I'm done screwing her she'll just be getting warmed up. She'll take care of you I'm sure. Or would you rather do your slave? I want to try her next."

Jake had his back turned and didn't see him. Darla did however. The glazed look of ecstasy in her eyes vanished and they grew wide in fear. Doubtless, she watched his grey eyes become flaming red.

Bristling with anger, Alonzo reached down and snatched Jake's hair. Yanking Jake from on top of Darla and abruptly ripping Jake's cock from her pussy. He turned the man to face him and clamped his hand around Jakes throat. Alonzo held the taller man above his head, dangling his feet off the floor. Desperately, Jake clawed at his arm, leaving deep gashes that Alonzo ignored. Instead he just shook Jake like a rag doll.

"Where is she? Where's Tess? If you've harmed her in any way I'll kill you," he said in a low but deadly voice. His grip tightened and he saw Jakes face start to turn blue. His nails grew, forming claws that dug into Jake's neck. His lips drew back, baring his fangs.

From the floor Darla answered. "If Tess is your slave then she's upstairs on the couch Alonzo. Tied up, but otherwise unharmed."

Still holding Jake in the air he looked down at Darla. "She's not there." He growled in menace.

"Then I don't know where she is. Probably hiding. Jake has been down here with me ever since he tied her up. Honest Alonzo. Neither of us hurt her." Her voice quaked with fear. He was certain Darla had never seen him this angry.

Jake ceased his struggles. His eyes were bulging and he hung limply, perilously close to death from oxygen starvation. "Remember what I said Jake. One hair harmed and you're dead." He tossed Jake across the width of the pool to crash among the lounge chairs and slide down the wall.

Turning on his heel, he raced up the stairs. Dashing into the living room he started calling. "Tess, Tess honey, where are you? It's me, Alonzo. Answer me please."

He stood silent, straining to hear an answer. Nothing.

Rushing toward the bedroom he called out again. This time when he became silent, he heard a muffled noise from the bedroom. He raced into the room but saw nothing. Then on the floor he saw her squirm out from beneath the bed.

Oh thank God. She's still alive.

More anger flooded into his veins when he saw her shredded sweats wrapped around the tape on her ankles. Stooping down he ripped the tape from her mouth. Moments later his sharp nails had sliced through the tape binding her ankles and wrists.

"Are you okay hon? Did they harm you?"

"I'm okay. Scared out of my wits, but okay."

He helped her to her feet. She wrapped her arms around his neck and clung to him, trembling in fear. "I will not let the harm you. I promise," Alonzo growled.

He heard a slight noise behind him. They turned as a unit to the door and he tucked Tess behind him. Darla stood in the doorway, completely naked. Both of her nipples were pierced. Her pussy was shaved smooth and on her pelvis just to the left of her fold was a scorpion tattoo.

He felt his eyes harden and knew they had turned red again. "I thought you were my friend Darla. I guess I was wrong. I never liked Jake but I tolerated him because he was your friend. No more. I should kill you both for coming into my house and threatening someone that means so much to me. Get out. Get out and take that piece of shit with you before I change my mind about letting you go."

In a soft voice, Tess spoke into his ear. "Don't hurt her Alonzo. If not for her I'm sure Jake would have raped and maybe killed me."

He felt his tension relax slightly. "Get dressed Darla." With Tess still clinging to him they brushed past Darla just in time to see Jake enter the room. He held the broken wine bottle by the neck and brandished the jagged edges at them like a knife. Jake had pulled on his pants but was not wearing a shirt or shoes.

Alonzo detached Tess's arms from around his neck and slid her behind him. "Jake I'm giving you a warning. Leave now and I will let you live. Try to harm any of us and I'll shove that bottle up your fucking ass before I break your neck. You know I can and will do it." A growl of warning and menace rumbled from his throat.

Jake's arm dropped. "Come on Darla. Let's go. I don't think Alonzo likes our company anymore. He'd rather spend the time sucking and fucking his human bitch."

"I'm not going with you Jake. But I do suggest you leave right now." Darla said from behind them.

Disbelief scrolled across Jake's face. "Fine cunt, stay here where you're not welcome. I'm tired of fucking you anyway. I'll put on my shoes and shirt and leave."

"Darla is welcomed to stay. You leave… now! Don't ever come near here again Jake." He stepped forward threateningly and Jake retreated.

59

Jake backed out the front door, sans shoes and shirt, got in his car, and drove away.

"Thanks Alonzo. After hearing what he planned to do to Tess he definitely isn't my friend anymore. I'm so sorry Tess."

Tess didn't answer. She just fixed Darla with a glare.

Darla stepped over to the couch, slipped her top over her head, and picked her skirt up from the floor.

After pressing the Velcro back in place she said, "I hope that makes you more comfortable Tess. I think seeing my bare pussy bothers you."

It was very apparent that seeing Darla's bareness did not bother Tess. Jealousy creased her face. However, Darla had provided her with an out for the pending confrontation. Thankfully, Tess embraced the *out* and avoided the tense situation.

"I'm sorry if I was staring Darla, it's not you're being shaved down there, it's… your scorpion tattoo. I was just imagining how getting that done must have hurt like hell. Its pinchers are actually located on you fold. "

Darla smiled. "Being too sore down there to have sex hurt even more."

"Jesus you two, can we stop talking about Darla's anatomy for a while," Alonzo groused.

"If you'll excuse me, I'll go downstairs and get my panties," Darla said, and left.

Belatedly, Tess realized that she was standing there in nothing but her torn t-shirt and panties. Her ripped sweats lay in a discarded heap on the bedroom floor. Jealousy overcame her embarrassment. She turned to him. "So, is Darla your girlfriend?" she demanded to know, in a harsh voice.

"No, Darla and I have been friends for years and yes we've had sex, but no she is not my girlfriend. Are you sure you're all right?" he asked, trying to change the topic.

It didn't work.

"So if she stays tonight, which I assume she is. Are you going to? Have sex I mean." She spat.

"No."

"Good!" she bristled. "I'm going to go in and take a shower. I feel really dirty." Without waiting for an answer she stormed into the bedroom and closed the door behind her.

He suppressed the laugh that rose to his throat and looked at the closed door that Tess had disappeared behind.

Jesus, retract those claws a little and settle your hackles wildcat.

****

He was just finishing sweeping up broken glass when Darla returned. Standing up, he saw Darla stood with her hands on her hips looking at him. "So what exactly is Tess, because you know I'm a little jealous? Is she your love slave? Your blood slave? Both?"

Rolling his eyes, he thought, *Not you too.*
Having two jealous women under the same roof could
be very dangerous.

"Neither. She's neither one."

"Alonzo I'm a little confused here. You're not
screwing her? You're not feeding from her? What the
hell are you keeping her for?"

"Long story."

"Um—hum. Well, since Jake was my ride and
he's gone I have all night for you to explain just what
she is."

"Darla—"

"Don't Darla me, we've known each other for
far too long Alonzo. I want to know just exactly what
she is to you."

"My friend."

"I'm your friend, but we do the wild thing on a
frequent basis and yet you tell me that you and she
aren't."

"We're not."

"So tell me, are we going to do it tonight for
old time's sake?"

"No."

"Geez Alonzo, I can see it in your eyes now.
You really care for this woman. Now I'm really
envious. I used to hope you and me…but I've never
seen that look in your eyes when you were talking
about me. Are you going to convert her?"

"Haven't considered it much. Certainly not without her being fully aware of the pluses and minuses."

Darla shook her head. "You've got it bad for her, real bad. You better think about it, because otherwise you're going to watch her become an old hag while you remain your handsome hunky self." Darla licked her lips and winked. "I'd be willing to help in her conversion, just remember that. In spite of being jealous I think I like her." She laughed. "She's spunky"

Chapter
~ 5 ~

"What's so funny?" Tess asked from the doorway of her bedroom. She had put on a t-shirt and shorts.

Darla glanced up at Alonzo quickly and then lied. "We were just talking about how all my luggage went down the road with Jake. Other than what I have on, I don't have anything to wear."

"I sure know how that feels Darla. Don't I Alonzo?" she said, directing her gaze to Alonzo.

"You know, I have pizza in the car if anyone is hungry," he said, dodging the question. "It's no doubt cold but we can warm it up in the microwave. I'll go get it."

Neither woman commented on his abrupt change of subject. Alonzo rushed from the room and they heard him go out the front door. Tess excused herself and returned from her room a few minutes later. "I don't have much that would fit you but I think one of my long sleep shirts might work for you to sleep in."

Darla took the offered item, folding it over one arm. "Thanks Tess. I usually sleep in the raw, but I can wear it in the morning when we have coffee. You're a lucky woman you know. I've never seen him care for a woman as much as he cares for you. And I've known him for…let's see. Damn, a hundred years now."

Tess did a double take when she thought about what Darla had just said. She was surprised at both the length of time and her comment about Alonzo caring for her. "You think he really likes me?"

Darla smiled. "Oh yes. He really likes you…a lot."

Alonzo returned and took the pizza in the kitchen. After eating a slice of pizza and visiting with Alonzo for a bit, Darla stretched and excused herself. Shortly after, he walked Tess her to her door, then continued toward his own bedroom.

Tess crawled under the covers but once again she lay wide-awake. It had been an eventful and terrifying evening. A soft knock on her door pulled Tess from her thoughts.

"Come in." The dim light of the bed lamp dispelled the darkness slightly and silhouetted him in the doorway.

"Can I join you for a while?" Alonzo asked.

"Oh yes. I wish you would. I'm still shaking and cold, I'm so scared." She pulled the covers back. "Please crawl in here with me. Just hold me. Just for a while please."

Closing the door behind him, he crossed the room and snuggled up against her back. To her disappointment, he only removed his shirt, shoes and socks. Even through her sleep shirt she could feel the wonderful heat from his body. The material of his jeans abraded her legs. He put his arm over her and took her hand.

"Thank you," she sighed and spooned even closer. "Alonzo, how many of your other friends are like Jake?" She felt him stiffen.

"Jake *is not* and *was not* my friend. Darla is my friend and she was his friend. None of my other friends are like him."

"Darla," she murmured. "Yeah she's pretty nice. I think I like her. She kept Jake busy to prevent him from molesting me."

They were quiet for a long time. She was beginning to think he'd fallen asleep when he kissed the nape of her neck and whispered in her ear. "Tess I really like you a lot. In fact, my *like* might even be considered love."

Smiling into the darkness, she felt his desire bulge against her butt cheeks. *He said he loves me. God in heaven he said he loves me.*

The word *love* scrolled endlessly across her closed eyelids. "You say that you love me and yet you won't make love to me. I don't understand Alonzo. I'm pretty sure that what I feel for you is love. I say *I think* because I've never felt this way about someone before.

67

When you left this morning you didn't chain me up. I could have easily left…but I didn't. I couldn't think of anywhere I'd rather be than here with you."

"I was worried that you'd left. I thought of how empty my life would be without you in it," he said.

She lifted his hand to her lips and kissed the back of it. She placed it under hers and on her breast then sighed.

"Will you excuse me for just a moment? I need to go to my room real quick. I promise I'll be right back."

"Promise you'll be back?"

"I'll be back."

He left the room and a few moments later he returned. To her delight he only wore his boxers. When he crawled in with her and snuggled up once more, she teased. "I was hoping you weren't paying a visit to Darla."

He teased back, "Why, do you want me to?" he asked as he looked into her eyes.

She squeezed his hand fiercely. "You know better."

"Just asking." Her grip on his hand tightened. "Tess, I want you so much. You're so beautiful, and if I do not have you soon. . . would you make love with me."

"God, yes! You don't know how much or for how long I've wanted you, but just as you said last night…we can't. I can't take another rejection like that Alonzo."

"I have already thought of the, and we can." Brushing her hair upwards he kissed and nibbled the base of her neck and then her ear.

"Oh God," she moaned as shivers raced the length of her spine. She sat up and he gently pulled her nightshirt up over her head, his eyes never leaving hers. The longing and desire were evident, even as he stroked his hands lovingly down her body and slipped her panties from her legs. In the next instant he removed his boxers and they too settled to the floor with her discarded clothing. When they came together again, there was nothing but heated naked flesh pressed against heated naked flesh.

Rolling her onto her back, Alonzo pinned her arms over her head and his lips skated over hers gently at first, but becoming more demanding. As their kisses deepened, he pinched her lower lip lightly between his teeth and pulled it down, sucking it in his mouth. She opened her mouth at his urging and he explored every inch of it with his tongue. He broke their kiss suddenly and tilted his head back to look down at her.

"Have I told you lately?" he whispered breathlessly.

She didn't say a word, she knew what was coming next and she wanted to hear him say it again.

"You're the most beautiful woman I have ever met," he finished.

And there it was. Her reaction was the same every time. Heart skipping a beat and stomach doing a flip-flop.

"If you think for one minute that I will ever get tired of hearing you say that, you're crazy," she whispered back and smiled.

Kissing his way down her breast he stopped frequently to whisper. "You're beautiful, you're beautiful, you're beautiful, and you're mine."

He suckled on her nipples until they were so hard she was certain they would explode. His hands seemed to be on every part of her body at once, making her skin sizzle with his touch. His tongue; magical on its own, seemed to be everywhere too, laving her breasts, sucking on her clit and delving deep between her folds. Her emotions soared and her body responded in an intense climax that crashed through her. Not bothering to pause, he continued with his glorious ministrations through her squirming and bucking. And just as one orgasm ended another began. Her entire body had become one giant erogenous zone and he knew just where and how to touch her.

She moaned and gasped, trying to gain some purchase Realizing it was helpless, she turned her head and muffled her scream into the pillow, not wanting to wake Darla. While she twisted and writhed beneath him, he held her pinned to the mattress with his body and plunged her into ecstasy over and over again.

"Alonzo, oh Alonzo," were the only words to tumble from her lips. She couldn't believe that she had cum so many times already and he hadn't even penetrated her with his cock yet.

"I want you inside of me Alonzo. I need you inside me. Now. Please," she whimpered and begged.

"Patience my love. Patience."

He crawled all the way on top of her gazing at her. He poised his cock at her heated and soaked sex. Agonizingly slow, he slipped into her. She wanted so badly to thrust her hips upward, to swallow him to the hilt quickly and completely, but he held her down with his hand making her accept his slow insertion. She felt the walls of her channel stretch to accommodate his shaft.

Finally she felt his balls come to rest against her. Reaching under her, he splayed his hand open across the small of her back and urged her into motion. His other hand held her arms above her head and he plundered her mouth with his tongue. Their hips began to rock slowly. Two pelvises grinding together at the pinnacle of each delicious stroke. His cock was buried in her, so deep, so wonderfully deep.

She heard him grunt in her ear and felt his cock pulse within her, another fiery climax roared through her. Her heart skipped a beat and then raced, pounding in her chest. When their climax faded, they lay together, motionless and in each other's arms, savoring the feel of their union.

"I'm not done making love to you yet beautiful."

Crawling from her, he flipped her to her stomach as if she weighed no more than a feather. So sudden was his move that she squeaked in surprise. Lifting her up, he positioned her on hands and knees and slipped into her from behind.

"God you feel so good. Fuck me Alonzo. Fuck me good. Fuck me hard." Somewhere in the back of her mind she was shocked at the words that tumbled from her mouth. She had never talked dirty when making love before. Somehow, it just seemed right that she did now. Making love with him was so different than it had ever been with others. Great and fantastic different. She'd never had such intense climaxes before. Nor so many during one lovemaking session. Her eyes were open but only thing they saw was an endless kaleidoscope of bursting fireworks.

"I love you. I love you. I love you." Flowed from her lips.

"You're so wet and tight Tess. I love you too," he returned.

She focused on the wonderful sensations flowing through her and forgot to move. Her body did not however, and with a mind of its own, it set her in motion. Her knees flexed, causing her to rock forward and back. First slamming herself back against his pelvis and then sliding up the length of his shaft, only

72

to slam back again. Each time his cock slipped deep into her, more fireworks burst in front of her eyes.

His hands lightly cupped each of her swaying breasts, following their motion for a while and then molding them, smearing the perspiration that covered them and all the time his wonderful, fantastic cock slid in and out of her.

This one is for him. I'm far too tired to climax again.

His hands smoothed down her sides and then latched onto her hips. Their grip tightened and again he grunted. She was wrong. She could climax again. As she did, one of his hands dipped under her and found her throbbing and swollen clit. Pressing and circling it, he prolonged her orgasm.

Her arms collapsed, her head sank into the pillow and she screamed into it as he held her ass up against him and unloaded. With each pulse of his cock, her body answered with ripples and tremors passing through her legs and belly. Slowly, he withdrew and tumbled to the bed beside her. Now that his hands no longer supported her, her knees slid backward and she sank the rest of the way to the bed.

"Still cold?" he asked.

In a dreamy voice she answered, "Uh—uh, not anymore. Were… how did you learn to make love that way?"

"I've had a lot of years to practice."

"Yes." The though of him being with others played through her mind but she blotted that thought quickly. "I don't want to know how many women you've practiced with. Just that you are with me now."

"Yes beautiful, I'm with you now, and I always will be."

Pulling her into his arms, they drifted into peaceful but exhausted sleep.

****

Tess woke. She turned and saw Alonzo beside her, watching her. Wonderfully, delicious soreness between her legs reminded her of the previous night. "Umm, morning lover," she breathed softly. "I hoped you wouldn't return to your other bedroom last night."

"If it is all right with you, I think I'll sleep here from now on."

"I'd like that. I'd like that a lot," she said.

"Then consider it decided."

"Guess we better get up, take a shower and fix coffee for our guest."

He tossed the sheet back leaned forward, and brushed his lips the length of her spine before smacking one of her naked butt cheeks.

"If you don't stop that, Darla's coffee is going to be seriously delayed." She giggled.

Alonzo smiled. "Go take a shower. I'll slip back to the other room, take one too and get some clothes on. Don't worry about Darla too much, she's a notoriously late sleeper."

74

He stood up and looked down at her while she rolled over on her back. "Um…"

"What is it my handsome lover?"

"I love your curly hair, but I would love seeing the beautiful pussy it covers."

She felt her eyes roll. *That has to be a man thing.*

"In other words, you'd like me to shave myself bare… like Darla?"

"I shouldn't ask. Its not—"

"Consider it done. The next time we make love, the grass on the playground will be gone." She winked up at him and smiled.

"Thanks' hon." He slipped out the door.

She crawled out of bed and strolled into the bathroom. After scrubbing and taking care of his request, she got dressed and went to the kitchen. Putting the coffee on, she fixed toast and sliced some fruit. She jumped in surprise when a female voice addressed her from behind.

"Good morning Tess. Did you sleep well?"

"Yes, thank you, and yourself?"

"I slept just fine."

She poured Darla a cup and set it on the table.

She watched Darla sniff the air. "Ah, somebody had a visitor last night."

"What? What are you saying Darla?"

Darla got up and walked around the table. Tess trembled when Darla placed a hand on her thigh and

75

pinned her in her seat. Leaning forward Darla sniffed in the direction of her sex. He was in you last night. I can smell him on you. Don't try and play coy with me Tess. From the way you're gingerly walking today, I'd guess he fucked you well too."

Tess felt her cheeks become flaming hot. *God, Darla how can you be so brazen? I'm about to die of embarrassment here.*

Darla laughed, her lips split in a huge smile. As if reading her thoughts she said, "I'm a vampire remember? I can smell sex very well… and he told me you weren't."

"We weren't. Not until last night."

"Well then, congratulations."

"Darla you and Alonzo—"

"Have we fucked? Yes. Are we boyfriend and girlfriend? No. Just friends, friends with benefits, but now that you're here we won't be doing the wild thing anymore. You needn't worry your pretty little head about that. The two of you are made for each other I think. I just wish you were a vampire. I wish he would conv— I'll shut-up now. I don't want to make him angry."

"What Darla. What did you start to say? Converted? How?"

"You need to ask Alonzo about that. I'm not going to say another word. I've said too much already."

They glanced up when Alonzo entered the kitchen. "So Alonzo, would it be possible for me to get a ride to town later and rent a car. It seems I'm afoot here," Darla said.

"Not a problem. Where you headed?"

"Back home to California I guess. I've been gone for some time and I feel a need to stay in my apartment for a while. Maybe check out the singles scene and find a new boyfriend."

"One better than Jake I hope," Tess chuckled.

"Yeah it won't be hard to find one better than him. Maybe I'll even try a human boyfriend for a change. I mean if you can find a sexy human like Tess here, I should be able to find one too."

They agreed on Darla's departure early in the afternoon. "Darla it has been so nice meeting you. I hope you'll come back and visit soon," Tess said.

Laughing, Darla cupped her cheeks so that their gaze locked to each other's.

"Tess it wasn't nice the way we first met, but I'm so glad we're friends now."

Clearing his throat, Alonzo broke in on the conversation. "Tess you need to go get ready and so do you and I, Darla."

"I don't understand. I'm just saying goodbye to Darla."

"I know, but you can do that at the car rental place. You're coming with us you know."

"Uh, no, I didn't know."

"Well now you do. I'm not leaving you here alone. Not for a while at least, and not with Jake out there."

"So, I guess I'm not your prisoner anymore? So what am I now, your sex slave?" she asked in pretended innocence.

Alonzo shifted uncomfortably and Darla put her hand over her mouth to hide her smile.

Tess let the silence drag out and then springing to her feet, went over and kissed him on the lips. "Darla knows what we did last night. As she reminded me, she is a vampire and she smelled your scent on me. I'll be your sex slave for as long as you'll have me." She kissed him again and giggled. "Now sit down and have coffee with us."

Darla wanted to hear the story of how they'd met, so, taking turns they told her. When they finished Darla's eyes misted over. "So Skag is really dead? You killed him Alonzo?"

"Yep."

"Please excuse me Tess." Darla got to her feet, stopped before the seated Alonzo and kissed him. "Thanks. Thank you so much. You have no idea how much this means to me."

"I'm a little confused here. Why does Skag's death mean so much to you? He was a bad man, but I still don't understand."

Darla turned to her, eyes still misted. "Skag killed my sister. Yes, she was a vampire too, but we're not completely invulnerable to injury, we just heal faster than humans. The bastard cut her head off. "

Gulping, Tess stood, put her arms around Darla and whispered. "I'm sorry about your sister, and I'm glad the man responsible for her death is dead."

Turning to Alonzo she said, "And that's why you were there at *Fantasy Dreams* you were tracking Skag?"

"Yes. That's what I do Tess. I track down and eliminate killers. Mostly vampires that have gone rogue. Ones that kill other vampires. There's a lot about me that you don't know - things I haven't told you yet."

"So Skag was a—"

"No Skag was human. I normally don't interfere with human actions...I hunted him down because of what he did to Darla's sister."

"So it doesn't matter how many humans a vampire kills as long as he doesn't kill other vampires?" she asked in instant anger. She watched him shift uncomfortably. "That's wrong Alonzo and you know it."

"I know that now. I'm sorry Tess. I was wrong..."

So we're nothing more than cattle in your eyes? Food!" She interrupted in a shriek.

"Tess, please."

"Why did you save me? I mean, I'm nothing more than a damn cow," she spat venomously.

Again she watched his feet shift uncomfortably. "To be honest Tess, I really don't know. From the very start, when you were serving me drinks in the club I knew you were special somehow. I don't know what it was. Your personality, your friendliness. I just felt attracted to you. When Skag attacked you, I just couldn't let you die if it was in my power to save you. Since then, living here with you, being around you, my attitude toward humans has changed."

Ignoring his words, she muttered, "A cow. I'm nothing more than a damn cow to you." Her vision started to blur as tears gathered in her eyes.

I will not let them see me cry.

"Wow," was all she said and shortly after that, she excused herself to start getting ready.

Just before she left the kitchen, she heard him say behind her. "Tess, you're not a cow, I love you." She shut out his words and after crossing the living room, slammed her bedroom door closed.

Chapter
~ 6 ~

Alonzo stared down at his coffee cup, oblivious to Darla's presence. Oblivious to everything around him, only feeling the misery that had welled up inside him.

Darla cleared her throat, making him aware of her presence. Dragging him away from his inner thoughts.

"I'll be dipped in shit. Things have really changed around here since my last visit. I never thought I'd hear those three little words come from your mouth."

"What three words?" he growled.

"Bull shit. You know damn well what three words I'm talking about but just to refresh you memory a little I'm talking about the words *I— love— you.*" She placed huge emphasis on each word. "Big tuff guy Alonzo, brought to his knees by a little girl. A human girl no less."

"Shut-up Darla. You don't understand." He grumbled.

"Oh I understand alright. I understand a lot more than you think I do. And don't grouse at me. I'm not the one you're helplessly in love with. I'm not the one that has you tied up in emotional knots. I wish you felt that way about me. I wish you'd said those words to me but it's not to be. But that's my loss." She sighed.

"Are my feelings so transparent?"

"Maybe not to someone else, but you and me go back a long ways. I knew you long before Tess came along. You've changed Alonzo. For the better I might add, and that's coming from someone who is pretty much as cold and emotionless as you were. That little girl has tuff-guy Alonzo wrapped around her little finger. Coiled up tight." She chuckled and motioned a circle around her little finger.

"I'm not wrapped," he groused.

"Oh yes you are." She smiled. "Take heart though. She's just as much in love with you as you are with her. I can see it in her eyes."

"She hates me now. She hates what I am, and she hates what I do. She hates everything about me."

"Again I say, bull shit! She may be a little pissed right now. The things you said, your attitude towards humans, one that I can see has changed, hurt her. She's trying to deal with the knowledge that there are bad vampires in her world. That there really are things that go bump in the night. That the things she once thought were just the stuff of nightmares, really exist. She has a lot on her mind right now and she's frightened. While she's thinking about that, she'll also come to realize there are good vampires too. Ones like you. The words you said to her before she left will go a long ways in making her forget your other words and her thoughts. She'll get over being mad. You'll see. She loves you."

"I hope you're right."

"I am."

"Darla, you're a good one too. And you aren't cold and emotionless. When we've had sex there were emotions involved."

She placed her hand on his. "Thanks that means a lot to me. You know, once upon a time, more years ago than I like to think about, I was young and innocent like Tess. I don't mean she was a virgin before you. I'm just saying that, compared to us she is young and innocent. It warms my heart to see the way she talks about you. To see the way her eyes glitter. God, I wish I had someone that loved me like she loves you."

"You'll find him."

She snorted. "I don't think it's from lack of trying. I've fucked a lot of men. I always seem to end up with the bad ones."

He looked deep into her eyes. Struggling for the words to say. "You know Darla, maybe you should try and steer away from being attracted to bad boys. Maybe you should be more… selective."

Chuckling, she answered. "I like sex… a lot. I know what you're trying to say— politely. I shouldn't screw every guy I meet. You're right. I need to change my tastes in men. The bad boys usually end up being just that…bad boys."

"Speaking of bad. You realize that Jake will probably go rouge. I may be hired to go after him."

"Don't worry. It won't hurt my feelings if you go after him. He wasn't like this when we first met. Don't get me wrong, he was a bad boy. Like I said, I seem to be attracted to that type, but he changed. He started talking about killing just for the thrill of killing. He never did though, at least not when we were together, but still… Just be careful if you go after him Alonzo. I don't want you to get hurt, but the hell with him."

"I'm relieved you feel that way. If the time comes, I will be careful."

"Okay, I'm going to go take a shower. I've really enjoyed our talk. I'm going to start looking for a different type of man. You and Tess are now my shining examples. I'm going to be more selective as to who I have sex with too. I'll just buy a vibrator to take care of things while I'm searching." She got up, leaned over, kissed his cheek and left the room.

Going into the living room he saw that the bedroom door was closed. He knocked. "Tess, can I come in?"

"Go away. I don't want to see or talk to you right now," she said.

"Please Tess."

"Go away," she said in a harsh voice.

"Fine," he said to the closed door. "Just remember, we're taking Darla into town this afternoon and you *are* going." He shook his head and walked away. Going into his room, he put on some swim trunks and went downstairs to try and swim away his frustration.

****

Tess sat on the bed lost in thought. Now that her anger had faded, she trembled in fear when she thought of his words. His uncaring attitude about human life. *How can he possibly be so callous towards human life?*

"I feel like his walking blood supply now. He's always been so nice to me though, and I'm human."

When he knocked on the door she jumped in fright at the sound of his voice. After she sent him away, she realized just how easy it would be for him to simply break the door down if he wished. She was powerless and completely at his mercy. He could do anything to her he wished and there wasn't a damn thing she could do about it.

He could easily snap me in half like a twig. She snapped her fingers. *Just like that.* She plopped back on the bed and cried some more.

85

The knock on her door caused her to sit up with a jolt. *Oh god, he's back. I made him angry before in the kitchen. He's going to kill me for sure now.*

In false bravado she barked out, "Go away Alonzo." And then under her breath she added, "Please."

"Tess it's me, Darla. May I come in?"

She groaned. So it was Darla. Another vampire. *The door won't stop you and I sure can't.* If they're going to kill me I may as well get it over with.

"Come in Darla."

Darla opened the door and stepped into the room. Tess studied Darla while she stood there. Darla wore her outfit of the previous night. Red high heels with straps that laced up to just below her knees. A short red mini skirt exposed the beginning curvature of her butt and fit low enough around her waist to expose the upper portion of her scorpion tattoo. The loose top exposed all of her belly and was cut so short at the bottom her breasts threatened to spill out from under it at any moment.

Dressed like that you wouldn't last for a minute in my neighborhood without getting raped. Then she thought of what Darla was. *No, I'm wrong there.* She was certain that Darla was almost as powerful as Alonzo. *There isn't a man alive that could make you do anything you didn't want.*

"I can see the look of disapproval in your eyes. Tess, I don't normally dress like this in public.

86

Seductive yes, but not slutty like this. You need to remember that when I came here yesterday I thought I was going to be partying with two men all night. I had every intention of acting like a slut and being fucked into oblivion by two handsome studs."

Darla was an enigma to her. They were so different. Darla didn't seem to care one bit who saw her brazen display of her body. Darla had not been uncomfortable being completely naked in front of her. Then there was the way she talked. Outspoken and she swore enough to make a drunken sailor blush. All these things and yet, she liked Darla. Liked her more and more as time passed.

"It's not my place to be judgmental. So, what do you want Darla? You didn't come in here to show off your bod. I've seen *all* of you before."

Darla came over and perched on the bed beside her. "I came in here to talk about Alonzo. I just came upstairs from watching him swimming laps like a mad man. You have him more frustrated than I've ever seen him and I've know him for a long time."

"Are we talking about Alonzo the killer? Alonzo that doesn't give a shit about people? Alonzo that thinks I'm nothing more than blood on the hoof? Alonzo the vampire?" she spat vehemently.

Darla reached out and took her hand. "Alonzo that treats you like a goddess. Alonzo that would kill anybody that harmed a hair on your head? Alonzo that has changed so much I can't believe that he's the same

87

vampire. Alonzo that loves you so much that his life would be empty without you? I think we're talking about the same vampire don't you?" Her voice was equally as vehement.

Darla cupped Tess's cheeks and snapped her head to the side so they were looking eye-to-eye. "You better face it girl. You're living in a world that has suddenly become filled with vampires. You live with one. You're a vampire's girlfriend. You have a friend that's one too. At least I hope we're friends. Saying that he doesn't think you are any more than blood is bullshit and you know it." Her voice had risen as she spoke so that it was nearly a shriek.

"Is he a killer? Yes he is. Not an indiscriminate one, but one just the same. His proper title is *Enforcer*. So deal with it. What is…is. Your only alternative is to go back to your former life, pretend we don't exist and live in misery. I know it would be misery, because you love him. I can see it in your damned eyes. Well news flash Tess, he loves you back."

Tess could see the anger that flashed in Darla's eyes and hear it in the harshness of her voice.

"I'm going to leave now. You can suit yourself. You can stay in here behind a closed door and feel sorry for yourself. Convince yourself how bad you have it, how afraid you are of the big bad vampires. Or, you can come out here and join us, be with the vampire that loves you and one that considers you one of her best friends." Darla got up and stormed toward the door.

"You are you know," Tess said. Darla stopped in the doorway and turned around.

"I am what?"

"A good friend."

"Good. I'm glad you feel that way. And Tess, please don't tell Alonzo about our conversation. I don't need him mad at me and thinking I'm interfering even though I am." Turning, she headed toward her room.

Tess sat on the bed once again, deep in thought. Their conversation had given her even more to think about. She knew she could never return to her old life. One that didn't have Alonzo in it.

"Go back to what?" she asked softly to the empty air. "Go back to being a cocktail server at the club? Have men rub and grab my ass every night and make all kinds of lewd suggestions to me. And me, put up with the pawing and the filthy suggestions just to get larger tips. To have Steve bug me constantly to loose a little weight so that I could get up on stage and take my clothes off?" She looked down at herself. Her thighs were less thick and her stomach closer to being flat. "Guess what Steve? I've lost weigh but you'll never see my body. Nor will any of your customers." Her mouth snapped closed.

Over the past months I've deluded myself into thinking of him as just a normal man I love. Not the vampire he is. I live in his world now. Things are

89

different. Just as Darla said, I'm going to have to deal with it.

Deciding to go talk to him, she headed for the basement only to have him come through the door into the living room. For a moment he gazed at her, then, shifting his eyes downward, continued toward his room. She cut him off. With effort she tore her gaze from his wet trunks that outlined his maleness deliciously.

"Alonzo can we talk?"

He nodded his head.

Standing on her tiptoes she brushed her lips to his and then stepped back. "I love you. Let me say that first. You're my entire world now. At the same time I'm afraid of you after learning you're a killer."

"Tess, I—"

She put her finger to his lips. "Please let me finish. I'm just going to have to learn to get past that. I'm also going to have to learn that you don't much care about humans. Myself excepted, I hope." She smiled up at him.

"I would never hurt you Tess and you know that. I'm learning to care about humans more. You've changed my attitude about that. As for the killing part, I won't talk about that part of my life with you. I'll try to insolate you from that part of my life."

"No… you won't. I want to know everything about you. Everything. Now, and in the future. If I'm going to be part of your life, I want to be a part of all of it."

"I love you Tess, but sometimes you get me so frustrated I just want to turn you over my knee and spank you."

"Sounds pretty kinky to me. I suppose you would pull my panties down and smack my bare ass."

"Oh yeah, spanking your bare ass sounds even better." His lips widened into a grin.

"Well then, if I misbehave, you have my permission to do just that. In fact, maybe I'll misbehave on purpose." She winked.

"I better go change out of these wet trunks," he said.

"Before you go, let me ask. Are you still planning to move your stuff into the bedroom? Are you still planning on sleeping with me even if I'm a bad girl sometimes?"

"Am I still invited?"

"Oh yeah," she said in a suggestive voice, blew him a kiss and turned to walk away. "O—h yeah," she said over her shoulder. She squeaked and then chuckled when he smacked her on the butt.

****

That afternoon they started driving Darla to town and just before leaving his driveway, they spotted her suitcases tossed on the ground. One of the cases had broken open and scattered her clothes. "Bastard,"

91

Darla grumbled while the three of them gathered the clothes.

"Well, look at it this way. At least he didn't take them with him," Alonzo told her. "I'll drive back to the house so you can change into something better suited for traveling."

"Nah just drive into town. I'll change back here while we're driving."

He and Tess looked at Darla and she laughed. "I have a long ways to drive and don't want to delay. Besides it's not like everyone here hasn't seen me naked before."

After renting the car and saying their goodbyes, Darla drove away.

Chapter
~ 7 ~

Tess woke when Alonzo brushed her hair to the side and began to kiss and nip along the nape of her neck and over her shoulder. That and his hand sliding along her side following her curves sent a shiver racing through her. She snuggled back, spooning tight to his warm body pressed against her. She felt like purring in contentment like a kitten.

"Good morning babe. Sleep well?" she whispered.

"I slept fantastic cuddled up to you. Better than I ever slept before you." His hand slipped down from her waist and two of his fingers traced lightly up and down along her bare folds. "I love you," he breathed into her ear.

Reaching down, she placed her hand over his and though not removing it, she stilled his fingers. "I love you back, but stop that. It tickles. It does other things inside me too, and I'm sure you know that."

"I can't resist, your skin feels so soft and smooth. Your skin is soft everywhere but particularly there." Two of his fingers dipped between her folds to stroke her inside."

She felt his cock stiffen against her and wiggled her butt to settle it into the crack of her ass. Her own arousal started to simmer within her. "Geez babe, didn't you get enough of me last night?"

"Never—I will never get enough of you. Making love to you has become an addiction. One that I have no desire to end."

Those heavy curtains over the window always keep it so dark in here. It only lightens a little in the daytime. I wonder what time it is.

While she pondered that question, his fingers were steadily increasing her need. She looked at the digital clock on the nightstand. "Oh my god Alonzo, it's nearly noon!"

Pulling his fingers from within her, she wiggled to the side of the bed. After sitting up, she dashed across the room and flipped the light switch. Instantly, brilliance flooded the room. Rushing from the door she padded into the kitchen and turned on the coffee to perk.

Upon returning to the bedroom she saw him sitting, but still in bed. "Get up old man. Get dressed. You promised to take me hiking today."

"I'd much rather sit here and enjoy the view."

She watched his eyes, and almost felt them as his gaze drifted over her naked body. "I'm sure I look like crap and I probably smell like a horse."

"You look beautiful as always. Even from over here I can breathe in the wonderful scent of sex that hangs heavy on you." He took the two fingers than had been in her and put them in his mouth. "Oh," he moaned, "and you taste so damn delicious."

She rolled her eyes. "You and that sensitive smell of yours. Your sweet talk is not going to get me back in bed. Even calling me beautiful won't get me there. I want to go hiking." Giving in slightly she added, "We can make love some more later…after we get back."

"Maybe I'll join you in the shower."

"No you won't," she stated emphatically. "I know what that will lead to if you do." She vanished behind the bathroom door and moments later stepped into the shower.

When she left the bath wrapped in a towel, he still sat in bed. "You're turn. Now get your lazy butt in there Alonzo. Even with my poor human senses I can smell you from over here. You smell of sex."

Chuckling, he went into the bathroom leaving the door ajar. "Won't work handsome," she whispered, knowing he could hear her even past the sound of streaming water. "I'm determined to go hiking." Picking up the blow dryer she flipped it on.

Alonzo left the shower wrapped in a towel. "Better, now get dressed," she ordered. Turning, she started riffling through dresser drawers and slipping on clothes.

She heard him sigh and go to his dresser. For a moment she watched him slip on shorts and pull on a t-shirt while she tied her tennis shoes. After finishing her bathroom duties and letting him take his turn, she put her hair in a ponytail and added just a touch of makeup.

They drank a couple cups of coffee and then he slipped on a backpack he had filled earlier.

"Kind of overkill for carrying a couple bottles of water don't you think?" She asked, indicating the pack. She arched her eyebrow and waited for him to tell her what else the pack contained.

He didn't tell her. Instead he just said, "I'm carrying it so you just don't worry about it."

Just before they left the house his cell rang. Alonzo answered, put up a finger to her and walked into another room. Tess couldn't hear the words but from Alonzo's raised voice she was certain he was not happy about what he was hearing. When he returned Alonzo had ended the call. He placed his cell on the kitchen counter.

"We won't be taking that. I don't want to be disturbed."

"What was that all about?" she asked.

"Nothing that I want to talk about."

"Alonzo—" She placed her hand on her hip.

"Not right now. I'll tell you later. Let's go." He grabbed her hand and led the way to the front door.

Hand-in-hand they strolled through the woods. Whenever she brought up the phone call he steered the conversion to something else and she at last gave up. She was certain he would tell her, but it would be at a time of his choosing. She dismissed it and turned her attention to the beauty surrounding them.

Spring had given way to early summer and though it was warm she knew that it was a lot cooler here in the mountains than down in the city.

"I never cease to enjoy this. Everything is so beautiful. The different shades of green leaves and bushes, the wonderful scent of freshness. I'm so content with my life here with you."

"I'm glad you're happy. Having you here makes my life complete," he said.

They entered the beautiful meadow where he'd taken her before. The profusion of wildflowers and their fragrance was intoxicating. He removed the pack and rummaged through it.

She became pensive.

"What's on your mind little one?" he asked.

"Oh, just remembering the first time you brought me here. Thinking about all those signals I sent out, asking you to make love to me. Signals you never got."

"Oh, I got them alright babe. I just ignored them—"

"You shit."

97

"I ignored them because I was resisting your charms. I was afraid to fall in love with you. I lost the battle though. I am hopelessly in love with you."

Smiling, she watched him remove a blanket and spread it out on the ground. Digging more, he removed a bottle of wine and a container containing sweet meats and cheeses. "Now I see the need for the pack," she said to him.

"How about a little picnic?"

"Sounds divine." She settled on the blanket and fixed a plate for both of them while he poured cups of wine."

Alonzo took a square of cheese and held it to her mouth. Mischievously she darted her head forward and pinched his fingers lightly between her teeth.

Alonzo cocked an eyebrow. "You're going to bite me little one? I don't think you have the proper type of teeth." He chuckled.

Using her tongue, she pulled the cheese from his fingers and licked them. After swallowing, she grinned and said, "Maybe not, but you do."

When they finished eating and drank another cup of wine they came together in an embrace. Kissing, caressing, exploring each other's mouths.

"Grow them," she demanded, breaking their kiss.

"Damn it Darla, I wish she'd never told you about this. I think maybe I'll make you two stop talking on the phone."

She giggled. "You won't."

"Probably not," he admitted.

"You won't."

"You just wait until I see her next time. Tess… don't you think this is a little kinky on your part?"

"When you talk to Darla next time you should thank her for telling me about this and not chew her out. It gets me so wonderfully aroused. At first when Darla told me about doing this, it scared me to death. Then when she explained what it did for her, the rush it provided, I just had to try it. I'm so glad I did."

"I don't like doing this," he said.

Time to turn up the temptation. She arched her back causing her breasts to jut forward and she twisted her torso side to side causing them to wave to in front of him invitingly. In satisfaction she watched his eyes follow them.

"Your words say you don't like this. The lusty look in your eyes tells me different."

"Tess," he protested, "When Darla does this it's with another vampire. You're not one I remind you. I might take too much."

"You won't. I trust you."

He grumbled in weakening protest and she twisted again. His eyes shifted from gazing into hers to focus lower.

"Please." She begged.

With a sigh, he nodded in agreement and she watched while his incisors elongated into sharp fangs.

99

When they stopped growing they were a little more than an inch long. She leaned forward, running her tongue over them and dragging it lightly over their sharp points carefully so as not to puncture herself. After savoring the feel of his fangs for a while she leaned back. Pulling her t-shirt off she smiled. "I had no idea what you had planned but I kinda hoped, so I didn't wear a bra." Gently forcing his head down, she nestled his mouth to the top of her right breast. "Drink." She demanded.

"Tess, I think you're getting a little bit addicted to this," he mumbled against her breast.

"So, I'm hooked. You have no idea how horny it makes me when I feel your fangs pierce my skin. When I feel you taste my blood. I know you won't take much, but damn, it feels so fantastic. You want me horny don't you? For later? Or you can take me right here, right now if you want. Maybe both now and later?"

She felt a slight pressure. No pain, just a little pressure, when his fangs sank into her. Closing her eyes, she enjoyed the wonderful sensation of him sampling her. Knowing that she was giving him a part of her in such a special way.

While he drank she talked and combed her hand through his hair. "I love it when you do this. It's such a turn-on for me. I love knowing I'm sharing something of me with you in such a unique way.

She didn't need to look down to know her nipples had peaked. She could feel they were almost bursting with hardness. It had nothing to do with the cool breeze caressing them.

Warmth and wetness pooled in her core while he drew out tiny sips of her blood. Her panties quickly became soaked. Even with her poor human sense of smell she detected the aroma of intense arousal rising from between her legs. She reached under his shirt and smoothed her hands up and down his back.

His fangs withdrew. She felt his tongue lightly lick across her breast and knew that he closed the tiny puncture marks he'd made. No trace of them would remain by the time they had walked back home.

Sitting back he spoke. "That's enough my sexy little wench. Put your shirt on. It's time we headed home."

Tess couldn't help puckering her lip. *It's not going to happen. Next time we come here,* she promised herself. *Next time it will. I'm certain it must have to do with that phone call.*

Looking behind her, she saw that the sun dropping below the mountain crest behind them. The trees at the top appeared framed in gold. He gave her his hand, helping her to her feet. Running her fingers over the rapidly fading marks where he'd bitten her, she slipped the shirt over her shoulders and helped him put things away.

101

Tess turned her back and faced the bluff edge. She hid the disappointment written on her face and tried to concentrate on the magnificent view in front of her. The valley below was already shrouded in shadow while the mountain tops beyond the valley were a shower of golden hues temper with the greenery of trees.

Alonzo stepped behind her and brushed her hair to the side exposing her neck. He trailed kisses up and down it while resting his hands on her belly.

He whispered in her ear. "I'm so sorry dear. I know you wanted to make love. I just can't get in the mood right now."

"It has to do with the phone call doesn't it?"

"Yes. I may have to leave soon. Then again they may find someone else to handle the situation. I'm not going to say more until I know for certain one way or another."

She didn't but she said it anyway. "I understand."

"I love you," he whispered and stepped back.

Her yelp of surprise and the splat sound of him swatting her butt echoed through the valley. He pulled her back into his arms again.

"You like doing that don't you? Does it make you feel man—ly…like you own— me?" she teased and suppressed a giggle. She wiggled her ass against his crotch.

"Yeah, I guess I do," he admitted.

102

"Guess what dear. I like having you do it. I like feeling possessed by you."

Alonzo spun her to face him and kissed her passionately. "You're mine and I love you." He led her toward the trail." Hands joined, they headed for home.

Just as they entered the door his phone rang. "I have to answer that," he said.

"I know. Go."

He dashed forward to get the phone. He was deep in conversation when she walked through the living room. Without a word she accepted the pack when he handed it to her and went in the kitchen to unload it. She'd started the evening meal when he entered the room. One glance at the somber look on his face told her the phone call had not been a social one.

"Bad news?"

"Tess I have to leave for a few days."

"Oh God. Do you have to? I know without your even saying it. A vampire has gone rouge. Can't they send someone else?" she pleaded.

"I can't, not again. I've turned down their requests ever since you've been here. Tess it's what I do."

"I know. I've heard you refuse. Knowing what your job is doesn't make it any easier to face though. Someone is going to die. I've put what you do to the back of my mind. Pretended it didn't exist. So has he killed a lot of other vampires?"

103

"She, Tess. The one I'm going after is a *she*. And yes, she's killed several vampires…and several humans too. I've got to stop her."

"Oh God it's a *she?* I never considered that both males and females could go rouge." She plopped down in a chair. "So when do you leave?"

"Tomorrow morning. I've got to fly to Seattle."

A groan rolled from her lips. "So soon? I know the answer, but can I go?"

"No."

"What will I do while you're gone? I'll be stuck here alone going out of my mind with worry. I won't even be able to talk to you."

"I'll be right back."

She watched as he left the room feeling totally dejected. When he returned he handed her a cell phone. "This is for you. I've already got my number programmed in. Please don't call me unless it's an emergency. I might be busy, but I promise I will call you at least once each day. Okay sweetheart?"

"Not okay, but better than nothing at least."

"You've been talking about planting a flower garden. Go to town. Get some plants and seeds and whatever else you want. That should help you pass the time. Here." He handed her a charge card. "Get whatever you wish."

After they ate she went with him to their room where he started packing. She watched when he took a bag down from the closet and saw that it contained all manner of knives, stakes and some items of which she could only guess their use. All polished to a bright shine and made of hardened wood."

"This is one thing about us that is true. We are susceptible to wooden weapons."

Their lovemaking that night was highly emotional and bittersweet. The next morning he loaded his bags into the Porsche preparing to leave. "I'll be home soon. You be good."

"I will. I don't have any choice. The one I'm a bad girl with will be gone." She smiled through her tears. "You be careful…please. I love you."

"I will. I love you back. I'll miss you babe." He leaned in for one last kiss then climbing behind the wheel and drove away.

Waiting until he had driven out of sight, she turned and went back inside. Into a house that was suddenly silent and empty. Drying her eyes she went downstairs started exercising and turned the music up full blast.

****

Even though she followed his suggestion and started planting a flower garden the days dragged by. The nights were even longer. Her cell phone became her constant companion. She never knew when it would be, but each day, as promised, he called.

Each time she greeted him with the same words. Ones that he returned.

"I love you. I miss you."

Five days passed and then he spoke the blessed words. The ones she longed to hear. "I'll be home tomorrow night."

"I can hardly wait. I'm licking my lips in anticipation." Reaching between her legs she caressed her sex. "I want to do wonderfully wicked things with you."

"Gotta go my little wench. I need to get a good nights sleep, finish up with a few details tomorrow and then fly home."

The next morning she drove to the city and shopped most of the day. Then she returned home and started getting ready.

Chapter
~ 8 ~

Darkness had fallen when he reached the house and drove into the garage. To his surprise she did not greet him when he stepped in the front door and entered the foyer.

I wonder where she is. I called her from the airport and told her I'd be home soon.

He stepped into the living room and found it to be dark. His night vision adjusted. He tossed the bag he held toward the coffee table and saw it skid over the surface before dropping to the floor. Dim flickering light along with soft romantic music drew him to the kitchen. When he entered the threshold he found one candle glowing brightly on the counter, lit the room.

Alerted by his footfalls, Tess turned to face him. "Hi lover. I thought you might be a little hungry when you got home but didn't know what to fix so..."

His face split in a grin as he took in the sight. She lay on the table. Shiny red spiked heels with attached straps that tied mid-thigh covered her legs. Matching red gloves ended just above her elbows. She wore the diamond earrings and choker necklace he had given her and nothing else. Unless you counted the whipped cream she had sprayed over her areolas and the cherry that covered each of her nipples. Her long hair hung over the table edge nearly grazing the floor and her arms were stretched above her head with her hands grasping a chair positioned backwards. A bottle of wine and a single goblet sat on the table beside her.

Stepping closer, he stood at one end of the table and looked down. Her legs were spread wide. His gaze followed the trail of whipped cream that went down the center of her belly and covered her folds. His grin widened when he saw that across her belly between her navel and her sex she'd spelled out in red cake lettering *Welcome home.*

"Oh, I so like what you've fixed for me. You look so delicious."

Walking around the table, he poured them a glass of wine. "I don't know whether to eat you or take a picture of you, you look both beautiful and scrumptious."

Her eyes grew wide in apprehension. "Don't you dare take a photo," she giggled. "Someone else might see it."

Starting with her cherry red lips he worked downward. Licking, swallowing, nipping and savoring the feast she'd provided him. He paused for a moment and took a sip of wine. Smiling he viewed his work thus far. Her breasts glistened where he'd licked them

108

clean, as did her belly. Holding her head up, he poured some of the wine in her mouth.

"You know that I will have to do a lot of swimming and exercising to burn off all this sugar I'm eating." He chuckled.

"Maybe you should stop then," she teased.

"Not a chance." Setting the wine goblet down, he started eating each one of the cake letters.

When he finished cleaning her sex of whipped cream on the outside, his tongue delved between her folds. His hands latched over her hipbones, his forearms pressed down on her thighs, holding her open and in place while he lapped at her sweet honey. He felt her tremble and watched ripples roll across her belly. Her hands came down and her fingers laced in his hair.

"Damn you're good at that," she moaned.

He felt her muscles tense, a sure sign she was close. Seconds later she confirmed his suspicions.

"Oh God I'm cumming."

A deep moan rolled down from above him. Tremors rippled through her thighs and more wonderful heated honey seeped from inside her. He rode her though her climax, and just as it started to ebb he began building her toward the next one. Sucking in her clit, he teased the tip of it with tiny flicks then rubbed it in circles with his tongue. He felt her tense again. Heard her gasp and strain against him as she tried to rock and thrust her hips. When she relaxed slightly he pulled her closer to the edge of the table. "Watch me. Watch me taste you," he ordered.

****

In compliance with his request, she propped herself up on her elbows with her hands clamped over the tables edge. She looked down and saw his head bob, felt his tongue twisting and squirming inside her, dragging her ever closer to what…her third climax. She could feel another building inside her. She so wanted to grind and thrust her pelvis. He maddeningly held her clamped in place with her legs splayed scandalously wide. The only thing she could do was rock on her butt cheeks. The surface of the table underneath them was slick with her sweat.

In a frenzy, she rocked back and forth. The orgasm ripped through her, agony and ecstasy mixed in equal parts. Tilting her head back, she closed her eyes and watched fireworks parade across her inner eyelids. Her heart raced and her pulse pounded in her ears.

"Watch me Tess," he growled.

Her head snapped forward and her eyes opened. Through hazy, blurred vision she watched him give her oral sex, seemingly intent on devouring her. Tiny short whimpers rolled from her lips each time his tongue plunged into her.

"Huh…huh…huh."

Her body tingled all over and her knees felt like jelly. The muscles in her arms trembled and shook,

110

threatening to collapse at any moment. The climax faded and still he consumed her.

In vain, she tried to draw away when his lips closed over her clit that had become ultra sensitive receptive to the slightest stimulation. His tongue scraped across its tip drawing an involuntary gasp of both pleasure and agony from her.

"Oh fuck. Do you realize how sensitive you've made me there babe?" she whimpered.

He didn't answer, but his stimulation increased. She squirmed in an attempt to pull away and protect her sensitized organ from further torture from his lips and tongue. His hands clamped down tighter on her thighs holding them wide.

Agony…ecstasy…agony…ecstasy. The mixed sensations crashed through her. Looking down, she saw her belly quake and her tits shake. Droplets of sweat covered her. Then the orgasm hit. It ripped through her, shredding all thoughts from her mind except extreme pleasure.

"Oh fuck!" What started as a deep moan tumbling from her lips, escalated into a scream of rapture. Her body shuddered and trembled and she surrendered completely, letting it take her into a place that only he could send her. Slowly the intensity of her orgasm ebbed.

In a near breathless voice she pleaded. "Please Alonzo…oh please…let me rest for a while. Let me catch my breath. God you're fantastic but you're

111

driving me insane." Her arms gave out. She fell to her back, raising her head at the last second to keep from banging it on the table surface.

His delicious torture ceased. She lay breathing hard and unable to move for a time. Rising up on one elbow she saw that he'd stepped back slightly. Her lip formed a pout.

"Here I provide myself as eye candy for you and give my body to you as a playground to have fun with. And you know every inch of that playground I must add. Yes, you've pleasured me as only you can. God, you've pleasured me. It just doesn't seem fair though, you're standing there fully clothed. Don't I get to see a little eye candy too?"

He grinned.

"I want to see you naked babe. I want to see that wonderful body of yours that I've missed so much."

Grasping his shirt near his neck he tugged it open, popping buttons off, and sending them flying. Shrugging it off his shoulders, he let it fall to the floor.

"Better?" he asked.

She sat up, perched on the edge of the table. "Better, but I want to see more."

He unbuckled his belt and opened his fly letting his pants drop around his ankles.

"More."

Hooking his fingers under the waistband, he eased his boxers off his hips and let them join his pants on the floor. "Satisfied now?"

"Almost. I want to feel you against me. You look so scrumptious. Come, come to me." She held her hands out beckoning him.

He stepped forward, picked up the goblet and they took turns sipping the wine. His eyes blazed with love when he looked over the rim of the glass at her. When it became her turn to drink she was certain hers did the same.

Placing the goblet to the side, he stepped into her arms, bringing his body against hers. Her arms circled him, holding him close. Their lips skated across each other's and their tongues twisted against each other's in a dance of love.

Gently pushing him back, she slid off the table. Leaving his lips, she kissed her way downwards. Her knees slowly bent, lowering her into a squat. She kissed and nipped her way through his chest hair suckling each of the tiny nipples perched on his pectorals. Her knees bent more as she kissed her way over his washboard stomach until she reached her ultimate goal.

Her lips parted and she slid his vein-covered shaft into her mouth until they came to a stop at its base. One hand rolled and fondled his balls gently while the other cupped over his ass cheek and held him in place. Slowly at first, her mouth slid up and down its

113

length while she drew him ever closer to orgasm. She heard him groan in pleasure. His fingers laced into her hair and she felt them tremble and shake.

Halting at its tip, she let her tongue play over it. Licking and sucking just the head and feeling it jerk and quiver in response.

"I see I'm not the only one that can bring on insanity," he said and another groan rolled from his lips. In answer she licked and sucked harder.

Feeling his cock start to swell further, she prepared for his climax. One of her fingers stroked along his scrotum urging it ever closer.

"Oh Fuck." He groaned and exploded. His ass cheek gripped in her hand, flexed with each pulse.

Hungrily, she swallowed each spurt of his seed when it pulsed into her mouth. Drawing hard, she pulled every drop from his shaft and waited until it went soft to pull it from her mouth.

Licking her lips she looked up at him. "Did I do good?" she asked.

With shaking hands he drew her upright. "That was fantastic," he managed before pressing his lips to hers. Breaking his kiss, he scooped her from her feet. "We can continue this in bed." Carrying her, he paused at the candle and let her snuff it out. Turning, he headed for their bedroom with her in his arms.

****

Tess opened her eyes and a smile came to her lips when she felt his sleeping breath tickle her neck.

114

Her long hair covered them like a veil. The two of them were even now, still joined, although he was flaccid inside her. Their arms and legs were wrapped around each other tightly, making it difficult to determine where she ended and he began. The residue from the whipped cream held them stuck together.

Though the bedroom was still dark she wasn't fooled and glancing at the clock sitting on the nightstand confirmed her suspicion. The time showed early afternoon.

But then it stands to reason we would sleep most of the day since we spent most of the night making love.

She had a terrible thirst that needed to be quenched. Carefully, she started to extract herself trying not to wake him. Slowly her skin peeled away from his.

"Good morning love," he whispered in her ear. Moments later he added. "Are you as thirsty as I am?"

"Parched," she replied. "If you'll unwrap yourself from around me sir, I'll go fix us something to drink."

He untangled and released her. Crawling out of bed she almost tripped over the shoes and gloves on the floor and started to pad out of the room. The soreness between her legs reminded her of their delicious activities during the previous night.

"I so love seeing that naked butt of yours," he said from behind her.

115

Sashaying her hips she replied, "Your butt looks pretty yummy too. If you want to shower first I'll go take mine after we drink."

Entering the kitchen she looked at the partially consumed bottle of wine and the small amount of whipped cream smeared over the tabletop. His clothes were in a small pile at one end of the table. A smile spread across her face in remembrance. Taking two glasses from the cupboard she poured each of them a glass of juice, setting them at the breakfast nook. She'd just seated herself when he joined her wearing briefs.

"Hi hot stuff. You look so delicious sitting there in the buff.

"Don't get any ideas on how we should spend the afternoon. I'm very sore and I have things to do. Clean the kitchen for one thing. Somebody or to be more correct, some*body's* made a mess here last night. I need to wash our sticky sheets and touch up the rest of the house, and work in my flower garden."

"I'll help." He volunteered.

"Thanks."

She followed his gaze down to the puffy folds of her sex. "Wow dear, that looks very sore. I'm sorry." Concern filled his voice.

Leaning over, she kissed him with lips that were nearly as swollen. "It is sore, but don't you dare apologize. It serves as a delicious reminder of the wonderful lovemaking we did last night. I'll be fine."

"Are you certain?"

116

"Yes. I'm sure. It's so great to have you home."

"It's good to be home. I could hardly wait knowing that you'd be here to greet me."

Changing the topic she said, "We didn't talk about it last night, we were too busy with other things. I trust that the problem you went to take care of has been resolved?"

He remained silent and so she added. "Remember, I told you that I want to be a part of everything in your life. The good and the not so good."

Clearing his throat he answered, "The problem has been remedied. She won't be killing others anymore."

"Meaning." She cocked her head to the side and arched an eyebrow, fishing for further information.

"You know well what it means. She's dead all right! Is that what you wanted to hear?"

"That's what I wanted to hear. Don't get mad at me. I love you. I want share everything concerning you."

Finishing her second glass of juice she stood. "Guess I'll go take my shower now." She hesitated, standing beside him and soon got the thing she waited for when he swatted her butt affectionately.

"Thanks," she whispered, flashed a smile at him and dashed from the room.

After taking a shower she dressed and rejoined him in the kitchen. She faked shyness when his gaze roved over her. His reaction was just what she

117

expected and hoped for, to her tennis shoes, baggy short-shorts and a sequined black bra. She'd gathered her hair into a ponytail and draped it over in front of her. Though she knew he was unaware, she had omitted wearing any panties.

"Just to keep you interested and make you work harder to finish. Then you can have me as a reward."

Licking his lips he answered, "Oh, I'll work hard alright, that I can assure you wench."

Cleaning the kitchen together, they moved into the next room. They decided she would do the living room while he cleaned the extra bedrooms. She stripped the bed and put the soiled sheets in the washer. Running a dust mop over the floor, she guided it under one of the couches. To her surprise she swept a shopping bag out from under the sofa and stooping over, retrieved it. Taking a seat she opened the bag and found the movies he'd purchased.

"Honey," she called out. "When did you get these?" While she waited for him to answer she sorted through the DVD's, Love story, The Way We Were, You've got Mail, and a newer one called Serendipity. Every one of them love stories. "Chick flicks" she knew he would term them.

He came into the room. "When did you get these?" she repeated.

Looking down at the collection in her hands he said. "I got them while I was gone and brought them home. I forgot all about them. There was something

118

delicious waiting for me in the kitchen last night, in case you forget. Where'd you find them?"

"Under the couch. I swept them out." Smiling up at him she said, "I guess we know what we'll be doing tonight."

****

They lounged on the couch together. Her legs were tucked under her and she rested her head on his bare chest. One of her arms circled his neck and her hands were hooked together. One of his hands caressed her arm lovingly while the other...the other was up to mischief, she reminded herself. After repeated attempts, she'd given up trying to pull her bra down to cover her breasts just to have his hand pull it up exposing them once more.

He squeezed and pulled on her nipples until both of them were rock hard and jutting straight forward. Using the tip of her own ponytail he tickled her breasts, causing her to wiggle and squirm. She was torn between her arousal and trying to focus her attention on the movie.

Reaching out, she smacked his hand. "Will you stop already," she said in pretended disgust, "I'm trying to watch the movie.

In answer, his other hand reached down and slipped through one of the leg openings of her loose shorts. Slowly, maddeningly, he began to stroke her folds. "I see you *forgot* to wear any panties," he commented.

119

"Forgot?" she grinned.

Two of his fingers dipped into her slick opening.

The sound that tumbled from her lips at this additional stimulation came out half moan and half purr.

"You say you're concentrating on the movie but you're wonderfully wet and warm."

"And I wonder why that would be. You've been playing with my nipples for the last thirty minutes. And now your fingers are driving me crazy."

"I can't help it beautiful. You turn me on."

With a sigh, she stood up "Aggravating man," she teased. "I can see that I'll have to take care of your desires before I can watch my movies in peace." Though she tried to keep her expression serious and sober, a giggle ruined her efforts completely. She unclasped her bra and shrugged it off, dropping it to the floor.

"Might as well get rid of it. It isn't doing much good up around my neck anyway. Then she untied the bow that held her shorts up and let them fall to the floor too.

Leaning down towards him, she unbuckled his belt and opened his fly. "Lift up," she ordered and when he did she slid his pants and boxers off.

"I see you have something all ready waiting for me." She said, running her hand over his erection lovingly. Spreading her legs wide she sat on his lap

120

facing him. Flexing her knees she rose, held his erection steady, and sat down, impaling herself to the hilt of his shaft

"Oh yes, you feel so good," She whispered. "So damn good," she repeated.

"Wouldn't you rather do this than watch a movie?"

"I have to admit, this is better."

"I thought maybe."

Leaning forward she whispered in his ear. "Grow em."

"Tess—"

"Grow em damn you." She giggled.

Leaning back she watched his fangs grow. "That's my man." Bringing her mouth down on his, she traced her tongue over his fangs. When she finished with that she cupped his head and forced his mouth to her breast. "Bite me...please."

His fangs sank into her breast causing almost no pain and just a little pressure, just as before, and soon she felt his tiny suckles as her blood flowed into him. The warmth and wetness in her core increased dramatically. The muscles in her pussy seemed to clench each time he sucked. Slowly at first, she began to slide up and down the length of his shaft with ever-increasing tempo. Soon, even the volume of the TV could not cover the wet slap of skin against skin as her butt slammed down on him again and again.

"Oh fuck yes!" she screamed out and tilted her head back. Her arms clamped around his head driving his fangs deeper into her while the orgasm tore through her.

"Suck me honey, suck me and fuck me." She felt him explode and relished the sensation of his seed surging into her. Knowing that he climaxed with her filled her with such joy and love. Stars marched in endless procession across her closed eyelids. She slowed. Her movements became jerky and finally she settled motionless on him and let him withdraw his fangs.

When she could move again she rested her head on his shoulder. "Wow, that was great."

"Let me close the fang punctures," he said.

"Leave them. At least for now. I like the feeling that you've marked me." She ran her hand over the tiny wounds and smeared the small amount of blood over herself. "I like the feeling that you possess me…that I belong to you."

"Honey, you only belong to me so long as you wish to."

"Then I'll belong to you forever." She kissed him.

When she stood, he lay down and patted the couch in front of him in invitation. She lay down in front and snuggled back tight against him.

"I love the feel of you skin against mine," he whispered. Reaching around her, his hand splayed open on her stomach and pulled her closer while he kissed and nibbled her ear.

"Can you reach the remote? If so, please start the movie over. I find that I've completely lost track of what was happening. Now that we've taken care of…other things maybe you'll let me watch it."

He chuckled and started the movie

.

Chapter
~ 9 ~

Tess lounged back on the couch watching one of the movies Alonzo had purchased for her. *I'll join him downstairs as soon as this movie is done. I wonder which swimsuit I should wear tonight for him?* Her thoughts were interrupted by a splintering crash at the front doors.

She was still scrambling to her feet when the door separating the foyer from the living room tore from its hinges and skidded halfway across the room. Two men entered the room. One she recognized immediately.

"Jake! What are you doing? You know that Alonzo will kill you just for being here."

In a blur of motion he stood in front of her. "I'll be the one doing the killing tonight. Where is he?" he asked with an evil look spreading on his face.

"Fuck you," she spat.

"I'll be doing that too…to you…and so will Mark, just as soon as we get rid of Alonzo. Then I intend to kill *you* slowly." Reaching out with his hand, one of his fingers hooked in the neck of her top. The sound of rending material loomed loudly as he tore her top from her.

She knew she was helpless against his strength, but at the same time, if they should succeed in killing Alonzo she was dead anyway. In a flash of motion her leg came up sharply and connected solidly with his groin. He bent over in pain.

"You human bitch!"

She leaped back, but not quite far enough to escape his glancing blow. He backhanded her across the face shattering her cheekbone and breaking her nose. The force of the blow sent her sailing across the room to slam into the wall about midway up. Dazed and hurt, she slid down into a seated position.

Stars spun before her eyes while she gasped for lost breath. An eye blink later Jake stood leering down at her, his eyes blazing red with fury. "You'll pay for that bitch. I should kill you now and fuck you after you're dead. But no I want to see the fear in your eyes. I want to feel your helpless struggles. Hear you beg for mercy." A cruel smile split his face, punctuated by his evil looking fangs. She saw that his hands were splayed wide with each finger ending in a long deadly claw.

Mark came up beside him. "Play with the human later, right now we need to find Alonzo."

"You're right. Spread out. Search up here for him. If he's not up here then he's in the basement. Later bitch. I'll return for you later."

She watched the two terrible vampires vanish down the hall. Heard them burst into each extra bedroom, the library and bathroom. They searched the bedroom she and Alonzo shared and the kitchen.

"He's not up here, so he has to be downstairs." Jake muttered.

Alonzo, why haven't you come up to investigate the noise? What are you doing?

The two of them went through the broken door and headed down the stairs.

What can I do? I'm sure Alonzo could beat one of them but two against one…I'm not so sure.

She felt hot stickiness trickle down the back of her neck and her nose bled profusely. An idea came to her, born of desperation. Struggling to her feet, she rushed into the bedroom. She dragged Alonzo's suitcase down from the closet shelf and tossed it on the bed. Frantically her fingers worked the latch until it opened.

For a moment, she viewed the selection of wooden weapons, trying to decide which ones to take. Deciding on two knives with six-inch blades she grabbed them from the case and dashed for the stairs in pursuit.

She knew it was a long shot. The chances of a human defeating a vampire were not good. *Still,* she told herself, *if it gives Alonzo an edge and he is able to kill them it will be worth losing my life.*

Her bare feet made no noise on the steps. When she reached the bottom she saw Alonzo facing the two of them. All three were crouched down searching for an opening. The two attackers had their backs turned to her.

Alonzo saw her, and saw the knives in her hands. She knew he would not approve of what she planned. *Tuff,* she thought. His eyes did not betray her presence. Dashing up from behind, at the last second she tucked one of the knives in the waistband of her shorts.

She knew that there was no way she could match the tremendous speed of a vampire if she faced him head on. Leaping on Jakes back, she locked her legs around his waist and hooked her ankles together. She ground her heel into his crotch. Her arm circled his neck in a chokehold and grasped her opposite shoulder, clinching her body tight to his. "Remember me!" she screamed into his ear and then bit down on it.

Moments later she plunged the razor sharp wooden knife in his side to the hilt. Pulling it out of him she drove it in again. Once…twice…three times she drove it in to the hilt. Jake shrieked in pain and rage.

Flopping to his back, he tried to dislodge her. She desperately held on, even as he landed on top of her and intense pain raced through her when several of her ribs cracked. Again she drove the knife home with a banshee yell bursting from her mouth. The blade broke off inside him.

He jumped to his feet and she pulled the other knife from her shorts, cutting herself in the process with its razor sharp blade. Hot sticky blood rolled down his side, spattered her bare leg and streamed down between them to drip on the floor. Blood gushed from her broken nose to roll down his neck and her arm. Reaching behind him, he grasped for her, but in doing this, he exposed his armpit. She drove the blade into it. Screaming in pain, his arm came down snapping the knife off at the hilt and leaving the second blade inside him.

He grabbed her arm and yanked it from his neck, breaking it in the process. He other hand pulled her legs apart and broke one of them. Pulling her from his back, he slammed her to the floor. She lay there, unable to move and knew he had broken her back. In addition she had a broken arm, a broken leg and cracked ribs. In silence she peered up into his vile facial expression.

"I'm dying bitch. Even now I can feel your fucking knife tearing at my heart. You however, will die first. I will drive my fist through that pretty face of yours."

Her shattered face stretched into a humorless smile when she saw a clawed hand reach into his hair and another one sink into his thigh. Alonzo raised Jake

129

from his feet and held him above his head. Dropping to one knee, Alonzo brought Jake down sharply and with an awful sounding crunch, broke his back over his raised knee. Alonzo reached out, grasped Jake by the throat, and ripped, tearing half of it out. With a final convulsive shudder Jake became still.

Turning her head painfully, she saw through eyes that were rapidly swelling shut that Mark lay on the floor nearby with his head twisted at an odd angle and half of his throat missing.

"Are they both dead?" she croaked.

"Yes, but don't talk beautiful."

"Good then I can die happy."

He knelt beside her. "Don't you dare die on me Tess. You hear me? Don't you dare die."

She knew she was dying. Knew she should say something profound just like in the love stories she liked to watch, but nothing came to mind. "It can't be helped. I love you Alonzo." She closed her eyes and blackness closed in.

****

"Tess! Tess!" Alonzo cried in anguish. He picked up her battered broken body and carried her upstairs. He gently laid her on the bed and placed his ear to her chest listening for her heartbeat.

Still beating, he sighed in relief. Her face was a wet, crimson, mass of blood. He saw the stickiness in her hair. Lifting her carefully, he found the deep

130

wound in her head and an ominous mushy feeling that told him she had a broken skull.

"Oh God, what am I going to do?" he whispered. "I can't let her die." He knew stopping blood loss, causing her body to mend injured organs and making new blood was within his power. Mending broken bones and a crushed skull was not. Tears streamed down his cheeks.

Slashing his wrist, he wiped some of his blood on her lips. Forcing her mouth open, he dribbled more down her throat. "It will keep her alive while I think."

Leaving the room, he flopped down in one of the living room chairs. Closing his eyes, he rested his head in his hands. Sitting back, his lips stretched into a grimace. Jumping up, he rushed into the bedroom, grabbed his phone and flipped it open.

He dialed a number and waited for an answer.

"Well hello there honey," Darla answered.

"Darla, I need you."

"Well I never thought I'd hear those words. What happened to Tess? Does she know? Don't tell me you talked her into a threesome. I'll never believe that."

"Darla, something has happened. I really need you here." He said, brushing her words of wit aside.

"I hear it in your voice. Something's wrong. What? Tell me about it." Her voice had shifted from light and joking to serious.

"I'll tell you when you get here. I need you to take the first available flight. I'll pay for it. Find one and book it. I don't care how much it costs."

"Something's seriously wrong. What's happened over there?"

"Please, just come. Call me back when you find out about the next flight." He hung up and sat waiting for her to call back.

He answered on the first ring.

"Tomorrow morning. Early tomorrow morning."

"Book it." He gave her a credit card number.

"Meet me at the airport."

"Darla, take a cab. I'll pay for it. I can't leave the house."

"Alonzo, you're really scaring me. What's going on—?"

"See you tomorrow. I've got to go." He hung up and rushed back into the bedroom.

Slashing his wrist again, he dripped more of his blood on Tess's lips and in her mouth. Her raspy breathing and the blood that foamed from her mouth told him that at least one of her lungs must be punctured. "Hang in there, baby. Just hang in there. Help is on the way." After tucking a stray lock of hair behind her ear, he caressed his hand across her brow and her cheek.

He curled up besides her, being careful not touch her lest he injure her more. Through the night he lay there, cutting his wrist frequently and feeding her more from himself. As the night progressed she started looking worse when multiple bruises stared to appear.

Glancing at the clock on the bedside stand, he saw it read five AM. He started awake when he heard Darla. "Oh my God Alonzo. What happened? Your front door is in splinters—" She stopped in mid sentence when she saw Tess. "Oh my God!" Her hand flew to her mouth.

"You know what we have to do Darla. I didn't want it to happen this way but we have no choice. It takes a male and female vampire to do it."

Nodding, she dropped her purse to the floor and crawled on the bed next to Tess on the other side of him. Their fangs grew. He bit into her neck and sucked her blood, leaving just barely enough to keep her alive. After it mixed with his, he forced Tess's mouth open. He bit down on his tongue and forced the bleeding organ into her mouth. Each time his tongue healed, he bit it again. He continued until he was light headed from blood loss and was forced to roll away.

Next, Darla bit into Tess. The blood she sucked was both his and Tess's. Withdrawing her fangs, she pried Tess's mouth open. "I've always wondered what it would feel like to kiss you Tess," Darla whispered. Tears began to roll down her cheeks. "But not like this. Never like this." Darla bit her tongue and started her kiss. They repeated the process over and over for several hours.

133

At last, the two of them sat up in bed. "We've done all we can. I just hope it wasn't too late," he said.

Darla looked at him. "Come on Alonzo, we need to get you something to drink. After that, you need to shower. You're covered in blood." Taking him by the hand, she led him to the kitchen.

He sat at the table. The world began to spin. "Darla, I feel so weak."

In a blur of motion she caught him before he hit the ground. "You've been feeding her all night haven't you?" she asked, easing him to the floor. "Then you gave her even more just a few moments ago."

"Yes," he admitted.

She ripped her top to the side baring her neck. "Drink."

"I can't."

"Drink damn you!"

"There's cow's blood in the fridge."

"What you need now is prime. My type of prime. I'll drink the yucky cow blood when you've drunk your fill, now do it." She pressed his head to her neck.

To weak to argue and knowing she was right, he sank his fangs into her and drank. She tasted so sweet. So wonderful. He stopped before he drained her dry and sat back. Darla crawled to the fridge and started drinking the cow blood to replenish what she had given him.

"Darla, I love you."

134

She rolled her eyes. "Yeah, yeah. Save the *I love you* for Tess. She's going to be fine Alonzo. I can just feel it."

"I mean it Darla. I love you too. I always have."

She looked at him again. "I think you really mean that, don't you?"

"I do. Things would never work between us. Being a couple I mean. I think you know that as well as I do. That doesn't mean I don't love you though."

Leaning forward, she kissed him on the cheek. "Thanks. Thanks for saying that."

They helped each other to their feet and hobbled into the living room to fall on the couch.

"I think we both need to rest and then we can clean this place up a bit. I mean your front door is a shambles. We may wake up and find a bear in here."

In a sleepy voice he answered. "If we do I'll beat the shit out of him. Or eat him…or maybe both. I'm in a really bad mood."

****

Alonzo jerked awake and the bad dream faded. Reality, which seemed just as bad, set in. Rising from the couch, he rushed in to check on Tess. She was still sleeping, but it sounded like she was breathing better and her bruises had started to fade. He felt a hand on his shoulder and saw that Darla had joined him.

"She looks better today. She's going to be fine. She's a scrappy little fighter," she said.

135

"Yeah, I agree. I know very well how scrappy she is. She killed Jake you know. Oh I hurried it along by breaking his back and ripping out his fucking throat, but he was already dying from the wounds she gave him."

Darla gave him an incredulous look. "I think it's high time you told me everything. There's nothing more we can do here but wait." Taking him by the hand she led him into the other room.

He told her the entire story. After that, he called and arranged for new doors to be installed. They went to the basement and started cleaning, beginning with the two piles of dirt, which were all that remained of Jake and Mark.

That night, Tess looked even better. Her broken nose had straitened, her shattered cheek looked less puffy and the swelling of her eyes was receding. Her color had started to return. She was definitely breathing better and her heartbeat was stronger.

"We need to clean her up now that it appears her broken bones are healed. She looks worse than she is. You still need to clean up too. Quiet frankly you're a fright to look at."

"Darla, you're covered in dry blood yourself."

"So, we'll all clean up together." Without any hesitation she started to strip.

He followed suit and while doing so continued. "If you'll hold her up I'll scrub her."

"If you'd prefer, I'll do the scrubbing Alonzo. I know how much you hate to risk harming her more. Maybe I would be gentler than you."

"No, I did it before, I'll do it again. Thanks just the same."

The two of them stripped the blood stained shorts and panties from Tess. Alonzo gathered Tess in his arms and the three of them moved into the shower. Darla hooked her hands under Tess's armpits. She held Tess with her back facing him and he washed her hair. Then Darla turned her and he scrubbed her from head to toe. Removing all traces of blood from her.

After toweling her dry they set Tess in a chair and dried themselves.

"Again, I find that I have no change of clothes here. This is getting to be an annoying habit." Darla said in an attempt at humor.

"Dresser, nightshirt," he said, pointing to one of Tess's drawers while he slipped into clothes himself.

"Lighten up Alonzo. She's going to be fine. Everything will work out. You'll see."

"I hope you're right."

"Trust me, I am. Woman's intuition."

Together he and Darla changed the bedding. He laid Tess down gently on the clean sheets, gave her a lingering kiss on the forehead and pulled the soft cotton cover over her.

"Thanks, Darla. I really appreciate all that you're doing. I'm an emotional mess. I don't know what I'd do without her."

Darla placed her hand on his arm affectionately and looked into his eyes. "Alonzo I'm glad to do it. I consider you family. You're the only family I have. Now, she's family too." To lighten the mood she forced a laugh. "I still find it hard to believe the scrappy little shit attacked Jake and killed him. She's a frail little human."

"She's so many things. Stubborn, hot-tempered, sarcastic and she loves to tease and torment me. I'm sure those are part of the reason I love her so much." Tears filled his eyes.

"She's going to be okay and now she's going to be around for a long time to tease and torment you."

Chapter
~ 10 ~

Tess opened her eyes and at first they refused to focus. Memories started to flood into her mind. Awful memories.

I must have been dreaming. I'm not in pain. If I were injured as bad as my dreams tell me, I'd be in terrible pain. Unless…unless I'm dead. Distantly she heard a voice.

"She's awake."

A face came into sight hovering over her. Her vision cleared more. It was a wonderful rugged looking face. One that she had grown to love so much. His lips were split in a smile that seemed to stretch from ear-to-ear. *Alonzo, its Alonzo's face.*

"Hi gorgeous," he said.

She reached up and placed her hand on his cheek. *My right hand. It must have been a dream. I remember that my right arm was broken.*

"Oh babe, I had the most horrible dream. I dreamed that Jake and another man broke in and attacked us. I was injured terribly and dying. I see now that it wasn't true. It was just a terribly bad dream."

Was that my voice? That weak, hoarse, croaking one? Maybe I'm sick.

Alonzo's smile faded.

"Am I sick? I sound so bad"

Another face came into view. One that she recognized. "Darla? What are you doing here?"

"You're going to be okay hon," she said and sat down on the bed.

Tess sat bolt upright. "It wasn't a dream. It really happened. I…I don't understand. I should be nearly dead. Unless I've been unconscious for a long time."

"I…" Alonzo looked at Darla and amended, "we, have a lot to tell you. A lot to discuss."

For the first time she noticed that the sheet had fallen when she sat up. After a moment of embarrassment she didn't care any more that her breasts were exposed to Darla. She also sensed that she was completely nude in her bed. One of them had undressed her. Maybe both.

"Suppose you two fill me in on what's happened from the beginning. I vaguely remember the attack. I want the entire story. First though, I need something to drink but I'm not thirsty for water. Something else that I can't quite put my finger on."

Darla jumped to her feet before Alonzo could. "I'll go get something for her to drink. You stay here with her Alonzo."

He started telling her about what happened from the beginning. Describing how Jake and Mark had broken in. How they came down to the basement. How they surprised him when he came to the surface in the pool.

"I must have been underwater when they broke in. I didn't hear anything until I surfaced and there they were. After scrambling from the pool I stood facing them. Each of us searching for an opportunity to attack. The whole time, Mark swore at me. It seems that the female vampire I killed was his lover. He and Jake had become friends and Jake found out I was the one responsible for destroying her. I don't know how he discovered this, but I *will* find out."

"And Jake knew where you lived," she supplied.

"Yes. Brought Mark right here. Jake hated both of us. I can only imagine what they planned on doing to you once they killed me."

"Awful things. Sickening things. Unmentionable things. He told me what he intended to do. I guess he thought it would increase my fear, and it did just that. His words terrified me. They also pissed me off. Made me determined to die first." She felt her face form a snarl when she remembered Jakes words.

141

"To continue, you came down the steps like some avenging goddess. A knife in both of your hands. The most god-awful expression on your bloody face. I must confess, I was both relieved and unhappy to see you."

He grazed his hand over her cheek. "God I love you so much Tess. I was frightened out of my mind. Afraid that I couldn't beat both of them together. Afraid of what would happen to you if I failed. Then you raced over and leaped on Jakes back. Screaming at him, cussing at him and stabbing him over and over. You took him by complete surprise. At the same time, your attack distracted Mark. I seized the opportunity and charged him. I had to shut out what was happening between you and Jake. What I was sure the outcome would be. I had to hope I could defeat Mark quickly and come to your aid against Jake."

She saw an expression of deep sorrow slide across his face and watched the moisture of unshed tears form in his eyes. "Unfortunately, Mark proved to be tougher than I hoped for. I finally defeated him, but you'd paid an awful price by my being delayed. Jake was dying. The wooden knife you plunged into him pierced his heart. He was just moments away from collapse, but he'd beaten you severely. With knees that wobbled, he stood over you and prepared to finish you off when I attacked. Tess, you defeated him. You, a tiny human woman, had defeated a tough male vampire."

142

"Yeah, but I was dying too."

"I know. Believe me I know. The thought that I was going to loose you ripped my heart to pieces."

This time she reached out, caressed her hand over his cheeks and wiped away his tears in the process.

"Anyway, I carried you up here put you on the bed and called Darla. She came, and now here you are, sitting up and on the road toward recovery."

Cocking her head, she looked in his eyes. "So what happened after Darla got here? You're not telling me everything babe—"

"Here you go hon," Darla entered the room and handed her a glass.

"Darla, I hate tomato juice. Where the hell did you find it in this house? I don't even keep the shit around."

"I made it myself. Now drink up hon. It's good for you."

From the corner of her eye she saw Alonzo stifle a laugh and put his hand over his mouth quickly. "Oh all right. I'm too thirsty to argue." Pinching her nose closed, she took the glass and downed the entire contents expecting to dread the awful taste of the juice.

It will serve you right if I puke this shit up all over you Darla.

To her surprise, it wasn't awful tasting.

"I've never tasted tomato juice like that. Sweet and yet salty, there's some other flavor too that I can't

143

find words to describe. You say that you made it. It's your own special recipe?"

This time Darla hid a laugh too. She covered her mouth with her hand. "What's so damn funny you two?" She saw the cut rapidly healing on Darla's wrist. "Darla you've cut yourself. What happened?" She heard the concern in her voice. And then it hit her like a slap in the face.

"Oh…my…God. That was your blood I drank. But it tasted so good. Oh my God… that can only mean that I'm…that I'm one too. That I'm a vampire."

Alonzo's face sobered. "Tess, I'm sorry. I had no choice. You were dying and I refused to loose you."

Darla leaned forward and kissed her on the lips. Leaning back she said, "I love you sis. You are my sister now you know. My blood is flowing in your veins and yours flows in mine."

"You have a lot to learn hon and Darla and I will be here to teach you. We'll feed you from ourselves until I can wean you to cow blood like I drink."

"A vampire. I'm a vampire?"

"Like he said Tess. He didn't have any other choice. You'll see, we're not so bad," Darla chuckled.

"A vampire. I'm a vampire." Instinctively she knew how. She willed her fangs to grow. She felt them and when they stopped growing she ran her tongue over them. They were not nearly as large as Alonzo's, but they were just as sharp.

144

My own fangs. Not his, she reminded herself.

She felt a smile spread across her lips as she became immersed in thought. *I wonder how it feels to bite? To sink my fangs deep into him. I wonder if it feels as nice as when he bites me. I can hardly wait to taste him. To see what he tastes like.*

She shook her head and concentrated on his words.

"One of the first things you need to learn is self control. Do not hurt humans," he told her.

"Don't hurt humans," she repeated without thinking. "Don't hurt humans!" she cried out in shock at her own words. She ran her tongue over her fangs again. "Oh-my-God, I'm a vampire."

Chapter
~ 11 ~

Tess pulled back the covers and crawled from the bed she'd been in for over a week. Darla and Alonzo were in the other room. One or the other of them stayed in the room with her most of the time. Each day they brought her a glass of "tomato juice."

At least I insist on calling it tomato juice but I know better don't I? I hate tomato juice.

Strolling across the room, she noted that her steps seemed different. She felt lighter on her feet, more powerful. Stopping in front of the full-length mirror she examined her naked body. Not so much as a singled trace remained of her recent ordeal. Only her memories remained of the pain and how broken her body had been.

That was in another life, she reminded herself. Things are different now. *Everything has changed. Well…not everything. He's still in it. The man I love so dearly. She's still in it. We're closer now than ever.*

"You're so damn beautiful Tess. I love you so much," Alonzo voice said from behind her.

Spinning quickly, she faced him. Rolling her eyes she said, "Yeah right. I'm a fright. Bed head, stubble growing in my armpits, my legs and…other places. I probably smell like a horse that has run for miles. Go away Alonzo. I don't want you to see me this way." Even as the words tumbled from her lips she felt the shiver of pleasure roll the length of her spine at his compliment.

"I need a shower. I'll meet you in the kitchen when I'm done. Now go." She made a shooing motion with her hands and smiled at him.

"Okay, if I must. Are you sure you don't need help…taking a shower I mean."

"I can take care of things myself. You're a naughty boy. I know what you have in mind."

"Can't blame me for trying, can you?" he said over his shoulder as he left.

She felt much better after her shower and shaving. Taking up the blowdryer she went to work on her long dark hair. When she finished it was still a little damp, but it shined with a healthy luster. It had grown so much that it nearly reached her butt.

No matter how much you like it Alonzo I'm going to have to trim it before it gets much longer. She caressed her fingers over the soft denuded skin of her sex.

What his lips and tongue do down there is just… baring it is a very small concession to make.

Placing her fingers on the spots on both sides of her neck, she smiled at the thought of the special kiss that Alonzo and Darla had given her. She knew that those kisses had saved her life, but they'd also changed it forever. Though the tiny puncture wounds were gone, she could still feel the warmth of them.

Maybe it is just my imagination.

Leaning forward she looked at her image in the mirror. A single thought passed though her mind. *Grow.* She watched as her incisors lengthened forming tiny fangs. The fangs of a vampire. She ran her tongue over them and scraped it lightly across their sharp pointed tips.

Yes, my life has been changed forever. Time to find out more about this new life of mine. Slipping on a pair of panties, shorts and a tank top, she padded barefoot to the kitchen.

"Honey your smooth strides on those fantastic legs of yours remind me of a graceful cat," Alonzo said. He pulled out a chair at the table for her and then slid a plate of toast in front of it.

Darla jumped up and went to the counter where she started pouring a glass of apple juice. "Alonzo you're going to have her ego built up so high we're going to find her impossible to live with," Darla said and chuckled. She finished pouring and set the glass in front of Tess along with the toast.

Tess felt her cheeks heat from his embarrassing praise. Looking at the juice and toast in front of her with distaste she said, "I'd much rather have some of that special "tomato juice.'"

A guffaw rolled from Alonzo's lips. "I'll just bet you would. I never thought I would see the day that my little Tess asked for 'tomato juice.' You always hated that type of juice."

She snickered, "But that 'tomato juice' is so special and so damn tasty."

Darla nearly rolled from her chair with laughter. "Honey, we'll give you some later, but for now you need to eat and drink what's in front of you. You need to learn to eat people food. Your body's been healing so we've given you a glass of our blood each day, but we need to start weaning you back. Normally you'll need nourishment of that type only once or twice a week."

Her lip puckered into a pout. "But the two of you taste so damn good," she complained. "So, besides the fact that you intend to starve me, what else do I need to learn about being a vampire?" she continued. Both Darla and Alonzo had refrained from telling her much during her recovery.

"We aren't going to starve you," Alonzo told her with a grin. "I guess I should start by telling you some of the negative things. Now that you are for the most part well, you're going to go through a period of being…aggressive and moody."

"Kind of like when you're having a period. All hormonal and shit, but much stronger." Darla added.

"And by the way, you won't be having any more of those."

Alonzo glanced at Darla, shook his head and grinned at her analogy. "It won't last long and Darla and I will be here to help you get through it. You're going to crave human blood. That you must learn to overcome. We can't have you feeding on the humans. You're going to find that you've become sensitive to sunlight. Damn, I'll miss that lovely all over tan of yours." He winked.

"I have an idea how that can be taken care of," Darla injected. "At first you'll find that you're sleepy during the day and wide awake at night. Gradually that will change as you get used to things. There are probably other things, but I can't think of them right now. I became a vampire a long time ago."

"Gee, it sounds like I'm going to be really hateful even hostile. I can't dine on humans, I need to avoid the sun and I'll sleep a lot. Are there any pluses to being a vampire?"

"Of course, you'll almost never get sick and injuries will heal amazingly fast," Alonzo began. "You'll discover that you can move very fast and that you have great strength. You have heightened senses of hearing and smell. But one of the best things you'll discover is that your life is incredibly long. How long, I don't know. I'm almost 300 for example. So, you'll remain your sexy, gorgeous self for a very long time.

151

On the negative side, you'll have to put up with me for a very long time too."

"I can't say that remaining young looking upsets me. Now as for putting up with you," She winked at Darla, "I'll force myself to live with that."

****

Tess threw back the covers and started toward the bathroom to take a shower. Gut wrenching cramps hit her so hard it doubled her over and brought tears to her eyes. The pain slowly subsided. She took a shower and got dressed. The nightmarish day was just beginning.

She couldn't explain it, but it seemed like every thing that either Alonzo or Darla said made her angry. More than once, she lashed out at them verbally. A little while later, she cried like a baby and begged them to forgive her. Alonzo tried to explain to her that this was part of what they had warned her about.

"Damn you! I need blood! I'm fucking starving to death! You're such an asshole to deny me going out and feeding," she raged.

He didn't say anything and Darla made herself scarce.

A few minutes later, she dropped to her knees begging him to forgive her and the words she had spoken. He pulled her to her feet and kissed her deeply instead.

"We'll get you through this, I promise," he told her.

152

Nodding her head and drying her tears, she put on her workout clothes and went downstairs. Two hours later, when she could barely walk, she came back upstairs and went in to take another shower. After she finished, she sprawled across the bed naked and sobbing.

Alonzo came in and helped her in bed, covering her with a sheet. Soon after, she dropped of into a sleep filled with terrible nightmares.

The next morning she woke with a ravenous hunger. Finding the car keys, she headed for the door, only to be met by Alonzo. "Please, Alonzo. Just let me go. I need to feed."

"I can't do that hon. Come on back into the living room. Maybe you should change and go swimming," he said in a calm voice.

"I don't want to swim! I want to feed. Damn you, my stomach is all twisted up in knots and growling like it hasn't had food in a fucking week!"

"I'll get you some blood from the fridge."

Suddenly, she seethed in rage. She felt her nails grow into claws and her teeth formed fangs. "I don't want fucking cow blood! It tastes awful," she shouted.

She lashed out at him in anger. Fast as she swung, he was faster still. He caught her wrist before her slap landed and when she tried to use her other hand he caught that one too. Stamping her foot in frustration, she turned and stomped away. Darla was just entering the living room to investigate the loud voices.

"I fucking hate you bitch!"

"And good morning to you too sis." Darla chuckled.

"Fuck you! I hate what you two have done to me!" She screamed at Darla as she stormed by. She stomped into the bedroom and slammed the door behind her, holding back at the last second and only making it rattle on its hinges instead of breaking into splinters. Tossing herself across the bed, she beat the cover with her fists in frustration. In time, sleep came and for once it wasn't filled with nightmares.

****

She awoke in a rage again. Her stomach was on fire. With a snarl, she leaped from bed and charged into the living room only to find him waiting.

"Don't try and stop me. I'm going out there to feed," she growled, nodding toward the door to the outside.

"No, you're not," he said in a calm voice.

Dropping into a crouch, she searched for any opportunity to get past him. The one that denied the thing she wanted most. To kill, to feed.

"Then if you won't let me past peacefully, I will hurt you." The words poured from her mouth in warning.

"Darla, I need your help," he yelled.

"She's sleeping. What, can't a big strong man like you control me? Someone that is half your size. You're pathetic Alonzo. I hate you." She taunted. Her hands formed claws and her fangs grew. Looking for any opportunity to lunge at him, she was taken by surprise when two arms circled her, pinning her arms to her sides and lifted her from the floor.

A scream of rage burst from her throat when she felt the naked body pressed against her back. She knew that no human could possibly stand up to her new strength.

But Darla isn't human is she? She's a vampire just like you.

Trying to reach behind her to sink her claws into the woman that restrained her, she twisted and squirmed. Her feet kicked in the air futility, seeking purchase on the floor.

Alonzo surged forward, wrapping his hands around her ankles. Together the two of them carried her writhing and twisting, downstairs. Forcing her back on the pool table, he trapped her body beneath his. Strong as she had become, she was no match for his unbelievable strength. She snapped at him with her teeth and clawed at him.

Two hands trapped her left foot, holding it motionless. Moments later she felt a restraint snap in place. In a short time her other leg was secured the same way. Redoubling her efforts, she ripped his shirt away in rags. Her claws sank into the naked flesh of

155

his back and raked across it. In satisfaction, she felt his skin curl under her claws as she carved deep furrows in it. It pleased her to hear his groan of pain.

Again, she lunged forward, snapping at his throat. He placed his hand palm down across her collarbone, forcing her head down to the felt of the table and holding her down. In desperation her claws sunk into his back again opening more furrows across it.

"Hurry Darla. She's clawing my back to ribbons," he shouted.

Darla grabbed one of her flaying hands and secured it to yet another restraint. Screaming in rage, Tess cursed at them. Her vision tinged in red with the fury that boiled inside her. Darla secured her last arm and Alonzo climbed off of her.

Twisting, squirming and struggling against her bindings, Tess glared at the two people that had tied her down through a haze of red. All manors of vile names rolled from her lips as she swore at them over and over.

"I love you Tess," he said in a calm voice. "You'll get through this, I promise."

"Ditto. I love you too." Darla smiled at her.

"I hate you! I hate you both!" she spat.

"Turn around Alonzo let me look at your back," Darla said, ignoring her hateful words

"Wow, she's a spitfire. She opened you good." Darla commented. "It's starting to heal but let me speed things up a little." She smoothed her hand over his back and Tess watched as the claw marks she'd made closed and vanished.

"Thanks," he murmured. "Well, sweet dreams my dear," he said to Tess, holding her twisting head in place on the table, and kissed her forehead. He and Darla headed for the steps and moments later the basement plunged into darkness.

She struggled against the chains that held her down, even though she knew it was useless. The fury in her gradually subsided. The burning flames in her stomach faded and remorse took the place of anger.

How could I have possibly said all those terrible things? Cursed and tried to hurt the two people that are my world. The two that I love more than life itself. Tears rolled down her cheeks and dripped on to the shredded felt beneath her while she lay in the darkness.

Still awake hours later she felt the sheet cover her. Opening her swollen, misted eyes, she sensed him more than saw him in the dark. "I love you Alonzo. God, how I love you both. I'm so sorry. I'm such a worthless bitch," she whispered to him.

"Shh babe. We love you too. You'll be fine."

His mouth came down on hers and they shared a sweet kiss.

"I'll stay down here. I won't struggle any more. You can leave me chained up like this for as long as

157

you see fit. God, I'm so sorry. Tell Darla I'm sorry, please."

"I will. You're going to be all right dear. We'll get through this together."

Again, he kissed her tenderly and then left.

The next day they released her. She spent the day moping around the house avoiding them as much as possible. Shame gnawed at her over her previous day's actions. At last, the long evening ended and she went to bed.

****

She awoke with a start. "It's fucking freezing in here. What Alonzo, did you turn the heat off or something?" she shouted into the darkness. She noted that he was not in bed with her. "I don't blame you hon. I'm an awful bitch. Damn… a freezing bitch."

Crawling from the bed, she jerked on a pair of panties and wrapped up in a heavy robe. Still cold, she stood on tiptoe, pulled down a heavy winter blanket from the closet shelf and wrapped herself up in that too.

Stumbling into the living room, she saw him asleep on the couch. "Did you forget to pay the gas bill or something? It's freezing in here."

His eyes popped open and he peered up at her. "It's late summer hon, remember? That you're having chills is a good sign though. It means that your body has almost finished adapting."

158

"Easy for you to say. You're not the one standing here with your teeth chattering so hard that you might break your fangs."

"A little humor too. Definitely a good sign."

"Humph," she snorted, turned and stomped back into the bedroom.

When she woke next, sweat poured from her. Peeling off the blanket and the robe, she found that she was still hot. Her panties were next to go. Walking into the living room, she saw that Darla and Alonzo were engaged in conversation. Both of them looked up when she walked by in the nude.

"Take a fuckin picture, it lasts longer." She giggled. "I'm going for a swim. At least the water will help me cool off.

Flipping on the light, she glanced up at the darkened glass roof. *At least the sun won't be beating down on me and increasing my discomfort.* She looked down at the beads of sweat dotting her skin everywhere she could see. Diving into the pool, she swam underwater to the far side.

Oh thank God. This water feels so cool.

She swam laps the length of the pool until she couldn't swim anymore. Crawling out of the pool, she collapsed into one of the lounge chairs and went to sleep. When she woke, she saw Darla sitting on one side of her and Alonzo on the other.

Slowly, she took stock of her condition. She wasn't burning up anymore, nor was she freezing. Her stomach wasn't tied up in knots or growling with hunger. Analyzing herself, she found that she was neither angry nor sad. She felt...normal. At least she supposed this was normal.

"I'm so sorry I was so nasty to both of you. I said some awful things. I hope you'll forgive me."

"Congratulations Tess. Your body has adapted. Oh and Tess honey, I love you." Alonzo smiled at her.

"I love you too Tess. We both know that you didn't mean the things you said. Though it was a long time ago, both of us have been through what you went through," Darla finished.

"How about some good old cow blood?" Alonzo asked with a laugh.

Chuckling she answered, "That still doesn't sound worth a shit, but alright.

Chapter
~ 12 ~

Following Darla's suggestion, Alonzo purchased a tanning system for Tess. Both women stood facing each other with their hair tucked under a shower cap per instructions.

"Told you he'd spring for it," Darla laughed.

"I had little doubt. He just couldn't handle the fact that now, since I'm a vampire, my golden tan would go away. He loves my all over tan."

"So, who's going to go first? You want to spray or be sprayed."

Tess thought about it and then answered. "You spray me first. That way if you screw up I'll be sure and return the favor. And Darla, forget about it. Don't you dare spray my sex and make it darker than the rest of me. Just remember that after you spray me I get to spray you. Just picture having one boob much darker than the other."

When Darla finished she looked at her work. "You look fucking beautiful if I do say so myself."

Handing the sprayer to her, Darla continued, "Okay, my turn. Be nice Tess. I was nice to you."

When they finished, both women looked at themselves in the mirror and decided they liked the new system.

"I wonder if I could get him to buy one for me to take home?" Darla giggled.

"Or, you could just get him to spring for a plane ticket and fly you out here every few weeks. That way we could visit and get a tan at the same time." Tess grinned.

"Now that doesn't sound like a half bad idea. Maybe both of us can work on him and get him to agree to that."

Even though it didn't require it, the two women ran around the house for the rest of the day nude. In doing so, they drove Alonzo crazy.

"An additional plus." Tess chuckled, watching Alonzo retreat to the basement to avoid gawking at them.

Darla laughed. "Should we follow and continue our torment?"

"I think we should, right after we have something to drink."

A few days later Darla announced her intention of going home. "You two don't need me here any more. I'm probably cramping your style." She winked at Tess.

"Huh," Tess snorted. "Darla, if I want to make love to my man and you happen to be where I want to do it I'll just do it in front of you." She laughed.

"And you don't think that would bother the shit out of me. Seeing you two doing the wild thing and me not getting any?"

She shrugged her shoulders. "If it made you uncomfortable then you could always leave the room."

"Uncomfortable? It would make me decidedly horny and I don't even have my friendly vibrator here to take care of things. No, it's time for me to go home. I must admit though, it's really nice to come here and visit. I mean, where else could I go to be among wonderful friends and get a new wardrobe to boot." She turned in a circle showing off one of the new outfits Alonzo had purchased for her.

"Yeah, yeah, Darla don't expect me to by you new clothes every time you come to visit," Alonzo said.

"Alonzo, you know that the only thing I would need to do, is ask. Maybe bat my eyes a little. You're a teddy bear. I can get almost anything I want from you. With the exception of Tess here, you love me the best. You even said so."

Alonzo shifted uncomfortably and both women broke out in laughter.

"Just don't get any ideas about having sex with him Darla. That's off limits." Tess reminded her.

"Yeah I know. I'd never do that to you Tess honey. Besides I've had him before. I'll always have those memories."

"I'm suddenly very hungry," Alonzo said in an effort to change the subject. "If you ladies wish to join me, I'll be in the kitchen." Turning, he quickly left the room.

"Ahh I think all the sex talk embarrassed him," Tess said. Again both women broke out in laughter.

"He doesn't stand a chance with both of us around," Darla said.

****

The next day they took Darla to the airport and after tearful goodbyes she left. Driving home, Tess turned to Alonzo. "I miss her already. We had some fantastic conversations."

"What about me? You and I talk."

"I know, and I love talking to you too. It's just not the same. Two women talking just aren't the same as a man and a woman."

"Give her a day to fly back and get settled back into her apartment Tess. Then call her. I know she'd love to hear from you."

"You know Alonzo, I'm not saying that I don't like talking to you. I do." Glancing at him from the corner of her eye, she grazed her hand up and down his inner thigh seductively. When he glanced over at her, she ran her tongue over her lips. "I like doing other things…besides talking…with you."

Taking his free hand she held it in hers. She kissed it and sucked on his fingers, wrapping her tongue around each one seductively.

"Tess," he growled.

"That's me. Your little Tess." She chuckled.

"While holding his hand with one of hers, she unbuttoned her blouse and slid one of her breasts out of the bra cup that covered it. She slid his well-laved hand onto her breast and held it there. You used to like touching them Alonzo. Do you still?"

"Tess you're being very naughty."

"Yes, but don't you still like to touch me?"

His hand squeezed her breast and his fingers pinched her nipple. "That answer your question?"

"Oh, yes." She moaned.

Her hand moved and cupped the bulge in his pants.

"Damn it woman, do you have any idea how hard you're making it for me to pay attention to my driving."

Giggling wickedly she said, "I guess you better try harder, because I'm not going to stop." Her hands became busy unbuckling his belt and opening the fly of his pants. She reached into his boxers and closed her hand around his erection.

"Damn it Tess," he complained when she began to stroke him.

"Quit complaining. Quit trying to pretend you aren't enjoying every minute of this."

165

Just as they turned into their driveway, she felt his erection start to swell and knew he was close. She clamped her hand tight, delaying his release. With her other hand she released the seat belt, hiked her skirt up around her waist, and scrambled to turn in her seat. She settled on her knees. Leaning across the center console while being carful not to bump the gear shifter she parted her lips and took him in her mouth.

She felt his leg muscles working when he disengaged the clutch and his other foot pressing against the brake. He brought the car to a gentle stop. She knew he could not shift into neutral. Her belly covered the shifter. The muscles in his right leg grew tight while the ones in his left relaxed. The car gave a slight jerk and the engine died.

Now that they were completely stopped and she knew he wouldn't wreck the car, she pulled her mouth from him and planted a kiss on the end of his swollen purple knob. "Cum for me my love. She lowered her mouth over his shaft once more and released the grip of her hand. His seed burst into her mouth and his cock pulsed as more and more surged forth.

A groan rolled from his lips. She could visualize his head rolling back and felt his hands twine into her hair. Suckling and licking she made sure to swallow each and every drop that he offered. When she knew she had drained him completely she sat back on her knees.

His glazed eyes turned to her. Looking him straight into them, she licked her lips seductively, "Damn you taste good."

"Hon, You have no idea what you do to me," he said as he started the car to finish driving up to their house.

"Maybe not exactly, but I have a pretty good idea."

He parked in the garage and she slithered out of the seat, smoothed her skirt back in place, and then sauntered slowly toward the front doors. When she heard the car door open and slam shut, she knew that he stood behind her.

She caused her hips to sway in an exaggerated fashion, knowing he watched her closely. Taking the key from her purse, she unlocked the doors. "Are you ready for the second round?" she called to him. Then, bunching up her skirt, she brazening pulled it up around her waist and flashed her bare ass at him. "You can have this," she slapped her ass. "There's just one thing old man...you have to catch it first."

She saw him lunge forward in a blur of speed. Shrieking in pretended fear, she dashed into the house. Calling over her shoulder, she taunted him. "You're fast dear. Very fast. If I were still mortal you'd catch me in an instant. But I'm not human any more, am I? You and Darla changed me. I'm a vampire just like you and I'm even faster. Don't you dare break the door down either, we just had it replaced." She reminded.

167

In the end, he caught her just as she had intended from the start. They made love for the first time on the living room floor. After that, they moved to the bed and continued.

****

"What a magnificent view," Tess said. She was stooped over with her eyes covered by the coin-operated viewer. She panned it from left to right and studied the city almost a mile below. "I'm so glad you brought me up here. I guess I didn't realize how large Albuquerque had gotten."

Alonzo stood behind her looking approvingly at her in her tight blue-jean cut-offs and crop top. "I agree the view is great. Two beautiful soft mounds. And though I can't see them right now, there are two fantastic peaks in the distance."

"Huh?" she said in a confused voice. "I think that is more of a mountain, not a mound and I've never heard mountains described as soft before. Besides, I only see one. Is that Mount Taylor?"

"Don't know that we ever named them."

"Alonzo where are you looking? I don't see any more peaks in the distance. I mean, from reading here Mount Taylor is about 80 miles away."

"Trust me, the view is breathtaking." Stepping up close behind her, he reached out and cupped his hand on her butt. "I'm looking at this mound and the matching one right next to it. We haven't named them, but we can if you wish."

Her cheeks heated. "Oh God, I should have known you weren't looking at the scene below. You're embarrassing the crap out of me." She glanced to each side to make sure no one was in earshot. "Don't you ever think of anything else?"

"Not when I'm around you. When I'm around you the only thing I can think of is you."

"Yeah, and no doubt trying to figure the best approach for getting in my pants too," she chuckled.

"Oh Yes, been there. Done that. It's heavenly. I can hardly wait for that experience again." He chuckled in return.

More heat rose in her cheeks and gathered in her core. She turned to face him with a brilliant smile on her face.

"And there they are, those wonderful, gorgeous peaks I was talking about."

She was certain she was glowing bright red by now.

He chuckled again when she rolled her eyes. Grabbing his hand, she led him down the steps. "Let's go to the curio shop and look around. We need to find something to distract you from my body. Remember, you promised to take me out to eat and then dancing tonight."

"Do you really think looking at curios will distract my attention?"

"Probably not. You have a one tract mind I think."

His mischievous chuckle told her he was fully aware of just how deliciously uncomfortable he was making her. "Only when it involves thinking of you."

"Damn you Alonzo." She grinned.

"Damn me?" he asked in mock innocence and arching an eyebrow.

"I love you." She sighed.

"I love you more."

Here at the mountain crest, two miles above sea level and with her scanty clothing, she should have been cool maybe even cold. Instead she perspired heavily. Her grip on his hand tightened and her pace increased.

"Behave." She giggled.

"Around you? Never."

They wandered through the shop and she picked up a couple of small items for souvenirs. Strolling hand-in-hand they came to his Porsche. After driving down the winding road from the observation crest they pulled into the drive and headed into their house in the mountains. She stopped him at the bedroom door.

"This is as far as you go sir. I have to get ready and then I'll let you in. It takes me longer. Besides, I know damn well if I let you in here, we'll end up in bed. Not that making love to you sounds bad, it's just that I want to go out first. I'm in the mood for dancing." Standing on her tiptoes, she gave him a brief kiss and then closed the door in his face.

He took a seat on the couch, picked up the remote and started surfing through the channels in an attempt to distract his thoughts, but he failed miserably. Nothing on TV could focus his attention elsewhere. Some of the channels he stopped on had the opposite effect. Hours later, the bedroom door opened.

Taking several strides into the living room, she stopped. "Well, do I look okay?" she asked.

Rising from the couch, he swallowed hard and let his gaze drift over her. "You're beautiful Tess. You always are… but tonight, you're radiant."

She had gathered her hair into a loose ponytail and draped it over the front of her shoulder. The diamond earrings and choker necklace hung from her ears and graced her throat, glistening in the light. Her lip-gloss was cherry-red. A silky maroon top hung loosely from two tiny spaghetti straps over her shoulders and exposed a goodly amount of her breasts. Her deep cleavage informed him that she wore one of the sexy pushup bras she had. The top ended a little above the waist and left just a little of her stomach exposed. Her black skirt, hemmed just above the knees, hung in folds.

Her feet were encased in low-heeled sandals with straps that circled her legs and tied just below the knee. A hint of delicious fragrance tickled across his nose.

171

"I thought about wearing a long dress, but since I want to go dancing after we eat I chose this one instead."

She twirled around, the skirt bellowed up giving him a momentary view of tanned legs, shiny black panties and bare butt before she came to a stop and it settled around her once more.

"I'm undecided whether to feed you or eat you because you look scrumptious."

Smiling, she teasingly suggested, "How about feed me first, dance with me next and eat me later."

"That, my dear, sounds like a magnificent plan."

"Then go handsome. Get ready to take me out. I'm starved…for people food, not people." She added.

Dragging his eyes from her, he went into the bedroom and got ready while she took a turn sitting on the couch.

When he returned, he wore dark blue sport pants and a sky-blue shirt. The shirt accented his broad shoulders and was unbuttoned in front just far enough down to afford a beginning view of his muscular chest.

Smacking her lips she stood. "Now it's my turn to hunger. You're making my mouth water dear." She ran her tongue over her lips gently to emphasize her words.

Smiling, he offered her his arm. "Shall we go my beautiful lady?"

172

She slipped her arm in his and together they walked to the car.

Chapter
~ 13 ~

"So where are you taking me? You've been very secretive handsome. You just told me that you were taking me out to eat and dancing afterwards."

"Just wait."

She puckered her lip and placed her clasped hands in her lap. "Patience is not one of my better traits hon."

"Wait." He chuckled.

After driving into the city, he headed north on interstate 25 and got off on the Tramway road exit.

"Won't you even give me a clue?" she asked. "It seems like we've been driving forever."

"Just a little further," He turned off 4th street and into the restaurant parking lot. "I hope you like spicy and hot. Sort of like you."

During their Mexican meal, Mariachis strolled through each of the dining rooms serenading. Tess sat back and sighed. "I can't eat another bite. The meal was excellent. I can only think of one thing I'd rather have," she hinted.

175

"If you're real good, maybe you'll get some of that later." He winked.

"And just what do I need to do to be *real good*?" she giggled.

"Are you about ready to go dancing?" He asked avoiding the question.

He drove them to a nightclub and as soon as they walked in, she turned to him. "I recognize that music. You're taking me Salsa dancing? I love Salsa dancing. I warn you though I'm pretty good at it."

"We'll see just how good you are."

They stepped onto the dance floor and after a partial dance they learned each other's moves. Their actions during the next dance were as if they were made for each other. As if they'd been dancing together since childhood. They twisted and shimmied, twirled and came together flawlessly.

Taking a breather, they sat out one dance. "I thought I was good but damn you're great at this. I'm impressed to say nothing of being flattered to be dancing with the best dancer here." She grinned and leaned closer into his arms.

"I've had a lot of years to practice." He stated simply.

"Yeah and a lot of different women too I bet. Dancing like this I'll bet you swept them right off of their feet and into your bed." When he didn't answer she jabbed him in the ribs.

"What?"

176

"You didn't answer me. I'll bet dancing like that got you a lot of women."

"Damn it Tess, I'm so aroused by you that I can hardly stand it. You're so sexy and vibrant. And those moves you make. You're good. Real good."

"Okay, I get the hint. You're not going to answer my question. Just remember who you're going home with tonight buddy." The music ended and soon the next dance started. They made their way onto the floor again and danced until just before the bar closed.

Being hot and sweaty, the cool night air came as a welcome relief when they walked out of the club. To her surprise he didn't head for home, instead he drove to a little bar that was just closing.

"Hi Ernie," he greeted the owner and introduced her.

"Hi yourself. Glad to meet you Tess. Go over there and sit in that booth until I can clear the place out."

A cocktail server brought them two glasses of water and joined the other server and Ernie in escorting the last of the bars patrons out the door. When they were gone, she returned to their table. "So what are you drinking," the waitress asked.

When she returned, she set their drinks in front of them and put stacks of coins on the table. "Ernie told me you needed these." She smiled at Tess. "You're a lucky lady. I'm envious." Turning, she walked away to start helping with the cleanup.

177

"So, are you ready to dance some more princess?" Or are you too tired?" He teased.

"Bring it on old man." She batted her eyes at him.

Taking her by the hand, he led her onto a small dance floor and fed coins into an old-fashioned jukebox. Soft slow music soon filled the air in the bar. They molded together and slow danced as if they were one body.

Just before she snuggled her head on his shoulder, she whispered. "I love you my handsome prince."

"And I love you back my beautiful princess."

The song ended and Alonzo dropped to one knee, his face just inches from her throbbing sex. Tess glanced around in panic afraid that he was going to take her orally right there in public. She relaxed a little when she saw there was no one in the room.

I don't care. He can have me whenever he wants and wherever he wants.

"Tess my love will you be mine forever? Will you marry me?"

Her eyes jerked downward at his words. She saw he was holding a small velvet covered box in his hand. *Did I hear right?*

He opened it showing her a diamond ring.

Oh God, I did hear right. He's proposing. Her heart skipped a beat and then pounded rapidly.

178

Butterflies surged to life in her stomach and fluttered madly.

"Yes. Oh God yes. Oh God." Tears streamed down her cheeks.

He took her hand and slipped the ring on her finger. She drew him to his feet.

"Tears?" he asked.

"Tears of joy. I love you Alonzo." She smiled.

"I love you more." He kissed the tears from her cheeks.

The music started and they swayed together again, oblivious to their surroundings. Only when Ernie cleared his throat did they realize he was there.

"I hate to break this up, but I need to go home."

Looking around, Tess saw that the two women were gone and only Ernie remained. "What time is it?" she asked.

"Almost 4 am," Ernie answered.

"Oh geez, we're so sorry for keeping you here. Aren't we Alonzo?"

"Yes. I'm sorry Ernie. Time just got away from me."

"No problem. It's usually this late when I get out of here. Watching you two fills my mind with wonderful memories of my Dorothy. Thank you." He escorted them to the door and they strolled to the car. Driving home Tess leaned over and kissed him.

"Thank you dear. Thanks for a wonderful romantic night I'll never forget."

"The nights not over yet my dear. We haven't made love yet."

Leaning back into her seat she sighed. "I can hardly wait," she said in a low dreamy voice.

When they got home, he gathered her into his arms, carful not to wake her. Halfway to the door she roused. "I'm sorry dear, I must have dozed off into a light sleep for a second," she whispered in his ear.

"Yes a light sleep, that's why you were snoring."

Nipping his earlobe she whispered, "I don't snore. That had to be your imagination."

"Then I've been listening to my imagination for the last 15 miles," he laughed.

When they stepped into the foyer she suddenly demanded to be released, "Put me down you beast. I don't snore." Standing on her tiptoes, she brushed her lips to his. "Bet I'm in bed before you." She giggled.

"I don't think so sweets."

"He watched her face sober and she pointed out the open door behind him. "Well you look at that?" When he turned, she shoved him out the door. Taken unaware, he stumbled into the yard a few steps before checking himself. Behind him, he heard a wicked laugh followed by the slamming door. Turning, he raced to the door and opened it just in time to see the one going into the living room close. Shutting and locking the outside door, he dashed across, opened the door and burst into the living room.

The door to their bedroom stood open but the lights were out. Flipping on the light he saw her lying on the bed in her bra and panties. Her clothes were scattered on the floor where she'd tossed them in her hurry to win.

"You cheat Tess."

"I know. But I had so much fun being a bad girl. If it makes you feel any better you can spank me." Rolling over she smacked her bare ass. "Go ahead spank it hon. Punish your bad little girl."

"Remember what I said about being good during dinner."

She puckered her lip in a pout. "So, maybe I'm a good *bad* girl. Come on babe get your clothes off and get over here. I'm hot for you." Rolling to her stomach again, she taunted him over her shoulder while wiggling her ass. "Come on babe what's the hold up. Don't you want to smack my ass? Don't you want to punish your naughty little girl? Don't you want what this little girl has to offer?" She taunted. "Geez my grandmother could get undressed faster than you."

He nearly tore his clothes off in his rush to join her. His clothes joined hers, scattered on the floor. The first thing he did when he crawled on the bed was smacking each of her butt cheeks.

"Oh yeah, just like that. I love it when you spank me. More," she begged.

Twice more he smacked her and then rolled her over. "You're such a bad girl." He said in a low throaty voice.

"I know and you love that I'm your bad girl." She beckoned him with her hands. "Come up here give your bad girl a little sample of your sweet kisses."

His mouth descended on hers and his tongue skated across her lips until she parted them and welcomed him in to explore ever corner. When he had plundered her mouth for a long time, his kisses moved down over her chin and grazed across her neck.

Busily his hands worked the clasp of her bra until it opened and exposed her breasts to him. He suckled and nipped each of her nipples until they were peaked and standing at attention. Moving down, he brushed his lips over her belly working from side-to-side seemingly in no hurry the reach the ultimate goal between her legs.

With a growl, he snapped the strings of her panties, jerked them from beneath her, and tossed them aside.

"Hey." She whined in complaint. "Those were new."

"Stop whining. I'll buy you new ones," he breathed into her folds and then kissed them.

"Oh fuck," she murmured and then shuddered.

He heard her moan and whimper when his lips closed around the swollen kernel of her clit. After sucking and rubbing its tip with his tongue, his mouth moved lower and his tongue dipped between her folds, lapping at the nectar he found there.

"God you taste so sweet," he whispered into her sex, not knowing if she heard his words. He hooked a hand behind her knee and drew it up and to the side, exposing the ultra soft skin of her inner thigh. Two fingers replaced his tongue inside her and his thumb worked her clit in tiny circles, pulling her closer to release. He watched as her eyes glaze over and knew she was close.

Feeling the walls of her channel start to tighten, he judged that the time was right. His mouth came down and his fangs slipped into her thigh. He felt it drive her over the brink.

"Oh Alonzo. Oh God." She moaned repeatedly.

The walls of her channel clamped around his fingers holding them tight within her. Tiny ripples rolled through her thigh. The small sips of blood he took were hot and tasted not only of the sweetness of her blood itself but the adrenaline and estrogen that were rushing through her veins with it. In his mind, he smiled, as her climax seemed to go on-and-on. When her muscles relaxed, he withdrew his fangs.

"Are you ready for the next one sweets?" he asked.

****

Vaguely she heard his question but it made no impression on her. She was still lost in the afterglow of the fantastic climax she'd just experienced. He briefly

183

paused while switching hands and then his other fingers slipped into her. They quickly took up the rhythm his other hand had established. Desperately, she tried to squirm away from that terrible, wonderful thumb that mashed against her clit, which had become ultra sensitive after her last climax.

"Are you trying to get away from me my sweet? I can't allow that."

"Dammit, You're driving me insane. I so love you." she heard herself whimper. It was a mixture of pleading both asking that his tortures cease and at the same time begging him to continue.

His hand clamped tighter around her knee, holding her in place. Fingers stroked her inside and caressed her g-spot. Her sensitivity only served to arouse her more when his thumb mashed against her throbbing clit driving her ever closer once again. She knew that the next climax would come much sooner and would be even more intense than the last. Her sex already tingled in anticipation.

In a delightful daze, she felt him pull her leg up and expose her left inner thigh. In the back of her mind, she realized that his fangs would soon sink into that one too.

God Alonzo, do you have any idea what you're doing to me? She answered her own mental question. *Yes you do, you know full well.*

"You're a terrible, wonderful man, my love," she whispered with her last coherent thought.

Her squirming ceased and she surrendered to him completely, letting him wind the spring within her tighter and tighter as he drew her ever closer to the brink of climax. Her orgasm surged to life, crashing through her like a runaway train. Her back arched and she cried out in ecstasy. She made sure that her thigh remained open, presented to him for the wonderful kiss she knew would come shortly.

His head came down and his fangs slipped into her thigh adding fuel to the fiery climax ripping through her. His hair brushed across her bare folds as he drew out tiny sips of the hot blood flowing through her veins.

She willed that the puncture wounds on her thighs remain long enough for her to caress them with her fingers. The tiny marks were evidence of his ownership of her body as well as her heart. After an unbelievable amount of time, her orgasm faded. Her arched back relaxed and let her sink to the bed. His fangs withdrew and she felt his lips brush her thigh in a sweet loving kiss.

The fingers in her and the thumb mashed against her stilled. Her racing heartbeat slowed at the same time the pounding pulse in her ears faded just like her roaring climax. The tension in her drained and she relaxed into a mindless, shredded heap of heated, sweating flesh.

"I love you," tumbled from her lips in tiny gasps. Words uttered in the heat of passion, but true nonetheless.

"I love you back," he returned and brushed his lips against her heated pussy that still twitched occasionally in the aftermath of the intense orgasm that had burned through her.

Unable to resist, she grazed her fingers over her widely splayed thighs feeling the puncture wounds from his fangs where he had marked her. Marks that he had left on her when he claimed ownership of her body. Marks that even now were fading away.

Until the next time, she reminded herself. *Until the next time he claims me as his. I can only hope there will be many, many next times.*

She whimpered in complaint when his fingers and thumb withdrew from her. He slid up and claimed her mouth with his. After a lengthy passion filled kiss he tilted his head back and looked her in the eyes.

"You are such a fantastic and good woman. I love you Tess," he whispered.

"I love you back Alonzo. You are my world."

"Remember dear, small sips."

"I'll remember and I promise. Small sips," she whispered. "I'm not going to risk losing the best thing that has happened in my life."

He bared his neck to her and let her sink her fangs in it. At the same time as her fangs sunk into his neck, she felt his wonderful cock slip between her heated folds. Slowly his hips began to rock. At the peak of each of his deep inward thrusts, she ground her pelvis against him and allowed herself to take a tiny sip of blood.

The slapping sound of wet flesh meeting wet flesh played in her ears as their tempo increased. *Tiny sips*, she kept reminding herself when she felt the urge to drink deeply. She knew that with time and practice, the sips she took would become automatic, but for now, she consciously had to limit herself.

"Oh god I going to cum," he said and groaned.

Moment's later, she felt his seed burst into her. "Now," he cried out. "Now let yourself take a deep drink."

She followed his instructions, taking a deep drink, and at the same time, a fiery climax consumed her completely. When it faded, both of them relaxed into boneless heaps still united.

"That was fantastic. Erotic beyond belief," she murmured after pulling her fangs from him and gasping for breath. Their mouths came together in a passionate kiss. Their arms circled each other and held on tight. Long after the fires of passion had passed they rolled apart to lay side-by-side. Smiling, she looked at a crack in the curtains and saw daylight shining through.

Rolling on her side, she focused on the shaft of sunlight. For a moment she glanced at the ring that circled her finger. The one that had replaced the collar around her neck. She knew soon it would be joined by a wedding band. Belonging to the man of her dreams sucked, wonderfully and deliciously, sucked. She held her hand out watching the ring glisten in the beam of light.

Alonzo smoothed his hands along her curves. "Regrets?" he asked.

"Not a one," she answered.

He nuzzled into her hair and kissed her nape. "I love you Tess," he whispered, his breath tickling her ear.

"I love you more." She spooned back against his warmth and sighed in contentment. His hand stilled, resting lightly on her hip. His deep breathing told her sleep had claimed him.

With a smile on her face, she joined him in slumber.

About the Author

G.E. Stills lives in the southwest with a loving wife two dogs and a cat. He has grown children with children of their own. In his younger years at school his teachers told him he had a vivid imagination if they could just read his writing. His long hand was/is terrible. Tongue in cheek, he blames it on being left handed and is very thankful for modern day word processors. While raising and providing for his family he didn't write for many years. Now that his children are grown he spends much of his time in front of his computer monitor. In his spare time he likes camping and cruising on a nearby lake in his pleasure boat.

He heeds the call of the many characters that pop into his mind and demand to have their stories put in print. Their tales are both serious and humorous. A multi-published author his stories cover many genres including contemporary romance, paranormal romance and science fiction. His stories are both erotic and non-erotic in nature. G.E. is the leader of a local writers group and in addition hosts a meeting of his own locally on fiction writing bi-monthly.

G.E. Stills loves to hear from his readers and can be contacted at any of these sites.

Web site www.gestills.com

Blog page http://authorgestills.blogspot.com/

Facebook Author page
http://www.facebook.com/AuthorGEStills?ref=hl

~ ACKNOWLEDGEMENTS ~

To My publisher SJ Davis for her patience with me in answering my many and sometimes silly questions.

To my book cover artist. Thank you for working your magic once more, S.K.

To my many author friends whose words of encouragement keep me writing.